GHOST BABY

GHOST BABY

MARGARET A. WESTLIE

SELKIRK

STORIES

Cover Design by A. Michael Shumate

Printed by CreateSpace, an Amazon.com Company

CHAPTER 1

Amanda MacIntyre hummed softly to herself as she sat on the steps and dusted the bannister of her new home. I love this old house, she thought. She slid her bottom down one more step to reach the newel post with her dust cloth. It's so elegant.

It was one of the older houses in Charlottetown, a two story Victorian built on Rochford Square, that by chance had not been turned into apartments in its declining years. With a little effort Amanda had returned gleam to the dark woodwork, and shine to the hardwood floors. I'm so glad Aunt Martha left it to me. She glanced at her watch. Oh, look at the time, I'd better hurry and change, she thought. Trudy'll be here in a minute and I don't want her to catch me looking like the maid on her first visit. She hurried up the stairs again.

The door bell rang presently, and Amanda could see Gertrude's copper curls glowing through the frosted glass of the front door. "Trudy, I'm so glad you could come! It's been ages. Here, let me help you with that." She swung the door wide and held out her arms to take some of Gertrude's packages.

"Thanks, Amanda, my arms are nearly broken. It was my own fault though, I shouldn't have tried to walk uptown to do my shopping. I always come back with more than I went for. C'mon Roderick, don't be shy. This is my friend Amanda, you may call her Mrs. MacIntyre." She ushered in a small boy by the left arm, his copper curls a mirror of her own. "Say hello, Mrs. MacIntyre."

Roderick pulled his soggy right forefinger out of his mouth and offered it to Amanda. "Hello, Mrs. 'Tyre," he said.

"Well, how do you do?" Amanda took the soggy hand in her own. "I didn't know you had such a grown-up young man, Trudy. How old are you, Roderick?"

"I'm almost t'ree," said Roderick, sticking three damp fingers in the air. "And I'm big for my age."

"Very articulate as well I see," she said to Gertrude. "You've got your hands full with him, I'll bet."

"Indeed yes, he's very b-r-i-g-h-t," spelled Gertrude, "there's nothing much gets past him, and he's got ears like a fox."

"I can hear lots of things," said Roderick.

"I see what you mean." Amanda laughed. "We're hoping to start our family soon, so I guess it won't be too many years before we'll be spelling things too. C'mon in, we'll have lunch in the kitchen, then I'll show you the rest of the house."

She led the way to the back of the house into a large, sunny kitchen. An old-fashioned wood stove sat side by side with a modern electric range. Sunlight bounced off the shiny trim on the stoves and was enhanced by the yellow-painted walls, so that the whole room seemed to glow with an internal light. Fire engine red trim on the chair rail contrasted cheerily with the yellow, and a lush English ivy framed the window over the sink.

"What a wonderfully welcoming room," said Gertrude.

"Thank you," said Amanda, "I've always loved this room, but Aunt Martha kept it painted white and I always felt that it needed more colour. When she left me the house, and I was free to do as I wished here, I decided to brighten it a little. You don't think it's too bright, do you?"

"Oh, no. It's just right, and I love that wood stove."

"We thought about taking it out, but you know these Prince Edward Island winters, and how often we have power failures. So we had the chimney cleaned and lined instead, and put in the electric stove to use in the summertime."

"That's a good idea, it might do for our house too. The cable to the mainland goes out often enough in storms and we always end up going out and staying with our friend Jim in Cherry Valley until they can fix it. He has a generator so he at least has lights. He also has a lovely wood stove in the kitchen as well as a furnace. He had company for two days twice last winter, and it's hard to get out there when it's storming. We have to make up our minds and go early before it starts drifting."

"Well, now, lunch is ready. I'll just make the tea. I made us a nice salad and we'll have some potted meat that I made the other day. Oh, it's so good to be home again!"

"How long were you and Alec in Toronto?" Gertrude sat Roderick on a chair on top of the thick dictionary that Amanda had offered her from the bookshelf behind the stove.

"We got married right after I finished training, and we went up then. Our honeymoon was our trip to Ontario."

Gertrude laughed. "So you're just now returning from your honeymoon!"

"You could say that," agreed Amanda.

"What's a honeymoon?" Roderick took a momentary interest in the conversation.

"It's a trip that people take right after they get married. It helps them get better acquainted."

"Oh." He digested this in silence for a few seconds. "What's 'quainted?"

"Acquainted," repeated Gertrude. "It means to get to know someone better."

"Like you and Mrs. 'Tyre?"

"That's it exactly," said Gertrude. "Mrs. MacIntyre and I haven't seen each other since nurses' training so we're getting acquainted all over again."

"Will he eat salad?" asked Amanda.

"A little, I think," replied Gertrude. "A peanut butter sandwich is more to his taste, though."

"Jam too?" Amanda rummaged in the cupboard for the peanut butter.

"A very small amount, he's not fussy about things that are intensely sweet. Unlike his mother."

"Me too," said Amanda. "I always have to be watching my waist line. Alec tells me I'm too skinny, but I know if I let it go, there'll be no stopping it 'til I'm as big as a house." She cut the sandwich into fingers and set it in front of Roderick. "My mother was that way, just enormous."

"So what brought you and Alec back to the Island?"

"Several things." Amanda arranged a marinated mushroom and carrot salad on lettuce leaves, then decorated the edges with thin-sliced rosy tomatoes. "We'd been thinking about it for a long time, but we could never afford to come. Alec had a good job with Social Services in Toronto. Well, actually, he ran the Willowdale office. He liked it pretty well, but then they cut the budget and moved a bunch of people and it wasn't the same anymore. They had as much work as ever and fewer people to do it. He got pretty frustrated." She paused for breath. "I was at the dentist's one day last fall, and I was leafing through one of those advertising-type magazines for tourism in the Maritimes, and there was a page of positions available. I glanced down the list to see what they had, and there was an opening for a Director of Social Services in Charlottetown. I was so excited I ripped the page out before I thought that it wasn't my magazine." She laughed. "I don't think they liked it, but it was too late then." She set the plates of salad down at each place and poured the tea. "I couldn't wait for Alec to get home, so I went to his office to see him. It was a circus! My mouth was still frozen from the filling I'd had, and I could hardly talk anyway, I was that excited. I finally just shoved the page under his nose and pointed. The rascal just said, 'We'll see,' and sent me home. I was disappointed, but I knew he was interested because he kept the page. He applied that night and they interviewed a few weeks later, and in the meantime Aunt Martha died and left me this house. I was her only niece, her only near relative for that matter, the rest are just third cousins down in Boston. It just seemed to fall into place. It was like it was meant to be. Have some cream." She passed the creamer shaped like a cow to Gertrude. "Anyway, Alec got the job, and we moved down in January. We only rented in Toronto so all we had to do was pack up and leave. I've been scraping and cleaning and painting ever since I got here. I love it!"

"I want some cow." Roderick reached for the pitcher, and got his elbow in his own small salad.

"Wait, honey, that's not milk." Gertrude grabbed his arm.

"What is it?" asked Roderick. "It looks like mik." He sat back on his dictionary as Gertrude scrubbed at his elbow with her napkin.

"It's cream, and it's very rich. A little goes a long way."

"What's cream?"

"It's the fat part of milk. It's what they make ice cream out of."

"Oh," said Roderick. "Can I have some mik, please?

"May I have some milk, please?" corrected Gertrude. "Yes, you may. Actually, I prefer milk in my tea too. Cream always seems rather thick."

"I don't usually use cream either but it seemed like a treat for a special occasion."

"Oh, do you want some too, Mommy?" He turned to Amanda. "We'd like some mik, please, Mrs. 'Tyre."

Gertrude rolled her eyes. "You see what I mean."

Amanda laughed. "I do see. You can't beat them sometimes." She got a new bag of milk out of the fridge and put it in its yellow plastic pitcher. She snipped the corner off the bag and poured it into a larger cow pitcher that matched the creamer. "There," she said, setting it down in front of Roderick, "A cow just for you."

"Oh-h," said Roderick in delight as he reached with both hands for the pitcher.

"Now, pour it carefully." Gertrude kept discreet hold of the cow's leg. "He's just learning to pour," she said to Amanda, shaking her head. "He thinks he can pour anything now."

Amanda poured more tea. "Are you ready for some dessert?" she asked. "I made us some Apple Brown Betty this morning. It's still warm, and it's delicious with that fresh cream." She took away the luncheon plates and stacked them in the sink. "The only thing about this kitchen is, that as large as it is, there's no place where we can conveniently put a dishwasher." She served generous portions of pudding into bowls and set them on the table. "Help yourself to cream."

Gertrude applied some cream and took a bite. "Mm, delicious, eh!"

Amanda looked pleased. "It was Aunt Martha's recipe. I fell heir to all her things, recipes included. Of course it took some deciphering to make it come out right. Her handwriting was always such a scrawl, and those old recipes with their pinches and dollops have to be seen to be believed. When you're finished we'll take a tour."

A few minutes later Amanda was showing off her new home. The ground floor had a large living room to the right of the front door, to the left was a dining room of the same dimensions that connected to the kitchen through the pantry. A closet behind the broad staircase to the upstairs had been converted into a washroom with a toilet many years ago, when Aunt Martha had moved in. The upstairs contained four large bedrooms, and a spacious, newly remodelled bathroom.

"This used to be the maid's room in the days when people could still afford to keep a maid." Amanda opened the door to a smaller room off the landing. "And look here, in this closet are the stairs to the attic. C'mon up, I've even cleaned up here." She started up the stairs pulling the string to the attic light as she went. The small windows at either end kept out most of the sunlight and gave the room an almost eerie feeling.

"We thought we'd fix up that room for a nursery, then when the child got bigger he could use the attic for a play room on rainy days. It has a lovely wood floor in it already. It needs new insulation, but that won't be hard to do, and with a little gyproc on the ceiling, and a few cupboards and some child-sized furniture it'll be just about perfect."

A cold chill went down Gertrude's back. "It'll be perfect," said Gertrude. Roderick began to squirm in her arms. "Can we go now, Mommy," he complained, "don't like it up here."

"In a minute, dear," said Gertrude, shifting him to her other arm. He reached out his sturdy boy arms to the far end of the attic.

"Pretty lady, pretty lady," he said, wriggling himself free of Gertrude's grasp, and running down the length of the attic. He stopped abruptly just before the end and looked around himself in a puzzled fashion. "Pretty lady gone."

Gertrude frowned and hurried after him. "C'mon darling, there's no pretty lady here." She turned him around and hastened him back to the stairs.

"Pretty lady sad," said Roderick, looking back over his shoulder to search the shadows at the far end of the attic.

"There's no one there, Roddy," said Gertrude. "It's time to go downstairs now. Come along." She grasped him firmly by the hand and started down the stairs. A somewhat paler Amanda followed them, turning off the lights and shutting the doors as she went.

The kitchen welcomed them back with its cozy brightness. "I'll make a fresh pot of tea," said Amanda. She filled the kettle and plugged it in. "Roderick seems sleepy, does he need a nap?"

"It is just about nap time for him," said Gertrude. "He can lay on the lounge there for awhile. He may drop off, and I can keep an eye on him there." They both avoided mentioning the pretty lady for the moment.

The kettle boiled and Amanda put down the tea, then set it on the warm burner to steep. It was difficult to think of what to say, so for the moment she said nothing. Gertrude settled Roderick on the lounge for his nap. The silence between the two women lengthened. The clock on the mantle shelf ticked on. Roderick slept. At last Amanda asked: "What do you suppose he saw?"

"Shadows probably," said Gertrude. "He has a very active imagination."

"Did you see anything?"

"No, but then I wasn't looking." She sat silently for a minute staring at her small son. "Did you see anything?"

Amanda breathed deeply. "No, but I wasn't looking either."

"Have you ever seen anything here?"

"No, not if you're thinking of ghosts. I don't believe in them, so I never look for them." She poured them each a cup of tea, and refilled the creamer with milk. "Help yourself to the 'cream.'" She passed Gertrude the cow. "Your mother had the second sight, didn't she?"

"Oh, she liked to say she did," said Gertrude. "I think, in her case, that it was about ninety per cent imagination."

"The old people believed in her, didn't they? I know the kids did."

Gertrude sighed. "There are a lot of gullible people in the world, especially among the very young and the very old. Mother had a gift of sorts, but it wasn't quite what she thought it was. She told pretty accurate fortunes on an individual basis, otherwise she couldn't predict what she'd have for supper. She worked very hard at creating an atmosphere. She said it enhanced her powers."

"Well, she did a good job of creating, then," said Amanda. "All the kids were convinced she was a witch."

"I know." Gertrude's lips tightened. "I spent a very lonely childhood because of it."

Amanda's bright blue gaze rested expectantly on Gertrude's set face, but no more comment was forthcoming. The clock on the mantle shelf whirred and groaned into life, tinnily striking four.

"My goodness, look at the time!" Gertrude jumped to her feet. "We must get going. I still have to walk home and I haven't done a thing about supper yet." She began gathering up their belongings. "Time to wake up, Roddy, we have to go home now." She bent over the drowsy child, who gazed at her with dreams still in his blue eyes. "Did you have a good nap, dear?" She sat him on her lap, and began putting on his shoes.

"I dreamed that the pretty lady was rocking me," said Roderick. "She was crying." He slid to the floor and stood leaning sleepily against Gertrude's legs for a moment. Gertrude helped him into his jacket. "It was only a dream, Roddy. Don't think any more about it. Thank Mrs. MacIntyre for your nice lunch."

"Thank you for my nice lunch, Mrs. 'Tyre."

"You're quite welcome, Roderick," said Amanda, "you'll have to come again." She showed them to the door. "I'm sorry about the pretty lady, Gertrude. I really think that it must have been shadows, I honestly don't know what else it could have been." She frowned, then laughed. "If there really is a pretty lady up there, maybe she'll babysit for me when I have little ones. She seems to like children well enough." She held Gertrude's packages while she arranged Roderick in the stroller. "You will come again, won't you?"

"It's my turn next time," said Gertrude. "We'll do it again soon. I'll give you a call, eh?"

CHAPTER 2

Gertrude hurried home, pushing a drowsy Roderick ahead of her in the stroller. It wasn't far, but it took her longer than usual because of all her packages, and part of the way was uphill.

"Pretty lady, pretty lady," Roddy sang to himself as he rolled along.

I wish he'd just forget about the pretty lady, thought Gertrude. Don's not going to like hearing about this. One psychic in the family is enough. She hurried up her front walk, and carried Roderick, stroller and all, up the steps. "Home again, home again, jiggity jig," she sang to Roderick as she unfastened his seat belt and helped him out of his seat. "There, Daddy'll be home in a few minutes, won't that be nice? Why don't you go and watch for him." She hung their jackets in the hall closet, stacked her packages on the hall table, and hurried out to the kitchen to begin getting supper ready. It's so wonderful to have a reason to come home, she thought, as she scrubbed potatoes and peeled carrots. Her thoughts wandered on. I know Don doesn't really expect me to be the submissive housewife, but it's just so nice to know he's coming home soon and that dinner'll be ready for him. She thought back to her many lonely years as the night nurse, working two jobs just to make enough money to keep her mother in the nursing home in the States. It's too bad that she thought she had to relinquish her Canadian citizenship when she went down to stay with Aunt Dolly, it would have saved me a lot of trouble and worry if I could have looked after her here, instead of having to go all the way to Texas every time she needed me. Not that she worried for the last few years with her mind in the state it was in. She put the vegetables on to boil, checked on Roderick, then began heating the large iron frying pan for the pork chops. Her mind wandered to all the work they'd done to restore the old house. The work was hard, she thought, but look what we've accomplished.

The eat-in kitchen had been renovated from top to bottom. The glass-fronted cabinets over the counter had been replaced with new modern ones with stained glass panels in the doors, countertops had been replaced with new beige sandstone coloured tops, worn cracked linoleum had been replaced with brown, basket weave, cushion floor, the surrounding pine board floors had been painted a darker brown to contrast with the cushion floor. I'm glad we painted the walls off-white yellow, thought Gertude. It has warmed the whole room, and the sunlight reflected from the stained glass doors casts such a beautiful light in the afternoon.

The front door slammed, and she could hear Roderick's running feet as he careened out of the living room shouting, "Daddy's home, Daddy's home!" He attached himself to Don's knees in a little boy bear hug.

Don grabbed him and swung him high in the air.

"Higher Daddy," squealed Roderick. "Up to the ceiling."

Don swung him high again. "How's my boy? Did you and Mommy have a good day?"

"We visited Mrs 'Tyre and saw a pretty lady. I had some cow from a real pretend cow, too."

Don sat him on his shoulders and walked down the hall with him. "Duck your head," he admonished as they went through the kitchen door. "Hi, Trudy, I'm home," he said as he bent to kiss her.

Gertrude laughed. "How could I not notice. Supper's a little late. I stayed at Amanda's longer than I thought."

"No hurry," said Don. "Anything I can do to help?" He deposited Roderick on the floor.

"No, just keep me company." Gertrude wiped off the table and began to set out place mats.

"What's Amanda's house like?"

"Beautiful. It was her Aunt Martha's. She left it to her when she died. Amanda's got that place shining like a bottle."

"When'd they get home from Toronto?"

"January. She's been cleaning and painting and polishing ever since." Gertrude flipped the pork chops and added onion slices, mushroom soup and a few shakes of Worcestershire sauce.

"They were real lucky, weren't they? Alec getting that job with the provincial government, and Amanda inheriting the house at just the right time, not to wish Aunt Martha gone or anything."

"Well, Aunt Martha was pretty old. Her health had been failing badly these last few years, so I guess it was no wonder that she went. Amanda said that she died at home in her bed."

"That's a nice peaceful way to go," said Don. "That's the way I want to go."

"Me too," said Roderick from his seat on the floor. "Where're we going?"

"Nowhere fast." Don laughed. "We have to have supper first." He stretched his arms and shoulders. "Mm, I have to get working out again one of these days, I'm getting stiff." He stretched again, then reached out a long arm and grabbed Gertrude around the waist. "C'mere you," he said as he deposited her small frame neatly onto his lap. "Am I glad it's the weekend!" He nuzzled her neck. "Do you smell good or what! Onions and perfume, my favourite scent!"

"Oh, you!" Gertrude laughed and wriggled free of his grasp. "Last week it was cod fish and pork scraps." She stuck a fork into the potatoes, it sank easily into the fluffy whiteness. "Supper's ready. You guys wash up while I serve."

Presently they were seated around the kitchen table. "Want to say grace," chirped Roderick.

"It's your turn," said Gertrude. "Do you remember what to say?"

"'Course I do," said Roderick. "I remember everything." He folded his chubby hands, bowed his head, and squinched up his eyes. "God is great, God is good, and we thank him for this food, amen. Mommy, do you suppose the pretty lady was hungry? I think she must have been. I think that's why she was crying." He picked up his small fork and began mashing his potato, skin and all.

"Who's this 'pretty lady'?" asked Don.

Gertrude shrugged. "I don't know, just something he thought he saw at Amanda's."

Don frowned. "Where did he think he saw it?"

Gertrude clucked her tongue slightly. It's going to be difficult to divert Don's attention, she thought. "Amanda was showing us the house, and he just saw some shadow or something."

"Yes, but where?" persisted Don.

"In the attic," said Gertrude.

"Did you see anything?"

"I wasn't looking."

"What were you doing in the attic, anyway?"

"Amanda was showing me a little room off the landing where the stairs go up to the attic. She said it used to be the maid's room. She wants to make it into a nursery, and the attic into a playroom. It really will make a perfect playroom when they get it finished."

"Humph!" said Don. "Not with 'pretty ladies' floating around in it, it won't."

"Oh, Don, that was just shadows. If anyone would know, I would, don't you think?" She ignored the memory of the shiver down her spine and the crawly feeling of her skin that had manifested in the attic.

It had been a week since Gertrude's visit. Amanda had finally shaken off the unpleasant feeling that had been engendered by Roderick's talk of the pretty lady. She still hadn't been back to the attic. I'm just being silly, she thought, but she didn't tell Alec about it. No need to upset him unnecessarily. She vigorously polished the big front window. What a glorious day! A fresh breeze from the Strait pushed fluffy cumulus clouds across a brilliant blue sky. The trees in the park were beginning to hide the Government buildings on the other side of the square. Not that they needed hiding, but they seemed so naked and indecently bare during the winter when the trees were leafless.

This is silly, she thought, reverting to her former reverie. Today is a bright day, I'll just go up to the attic and stop this nonsense once and for all. She put down her polishing rag and started up the stairs. Her feet slowed of their own accord as she neared the top. I can't do this. She went slowly into the small bedroom and stood staring at the door to the attic for some minutes. I'm being a nervous Nellie, she scolded herself. She squared her shoulders, threw open the door, and turned on the light. She took a step upward, then another, then finally took a deep breath and ran to the top. Well, I'm here, she thought, with tightly closed eyelids. Open your eyes, you ninny, you can't see if anything's amiss if you don't look. She opened her eyes and slowly turned her head, leaving the far end of the attic for last. And you're the one who doesn't believe in ghosts! She forced herself to look into the last corners. Nothing.

See, silly! There's nothing here, and there never was. She turned to go back downstairs. A sudden draft slammed the door at the foot of the stairs. Amanda shrieked and went down the steps two at a time, through the door, across the maid's room, and down the main staircase, collapsing in a breathless heap on the bottom step in the downstairs foyer.

A shadow appeared behind the frosted glass of the front door, and the knob rattled. Amanda held her breath and gathered herself to run again, as she waited, watching the door swing open.

"Hi, honey, I'm home early."

Amanda let out her breath in a rush and leaped to her feet. "Oh, I'm so glad to see you!" She flung her arms around Alec's skinny body.

Alec set his briefcase on the floor and returned her embrace. "Whatever's the matter, Amanda, you're as white as a sheet!"

She quieted herself a little in the security of his arms. "I'm just being silly. I was up in the attic looking around and the door slammed shut at the bottom of the stairs, and it scared me, that's all." She snuggled deeper into his embrace. "Let's go out for supper."

"Just my plan," said Alec. "I thought we might go to that nice fish restaurant in Rustico. They're open on the weekends now. I need to have a wash and change my clothes before we go. Why don't you put on that pink cashmere sweater that makes you look like a kitten."

"The one you like so well?"

"Yeah, that one."

An hour later they took their places at a quiet table by the window overlooking the harbour at Rustico. Fishing boats laden with lobster traps rode on the shallow water waiting for the full high tide at two a.m. Overhead seagulls wheeled and balanced on the breeze ready to follow the boats to sea. The sun was setting and wrapped everything in a golden glow. It would be a moonlit night. The scene was framed by sheer white curtains held back by lace ties. The ceiling was an old fashioned stamped tin that had been painted cream to match the walls. In contrast, the wainscoting was a rich maroon. Paintings of local scenes of fishing boats and lobster traps, and framed in ornate frames salvaged from estate sales, were hung here and there. They were signed by local artists, some of national fame.

Alec opened his menu. "I know what I'm going to have without even looking." He scanned down the list of dishes. "Here it is, Sole Almondine, with rice pilaf and vegetables."

"My mouth's watering for some salt cod and pork scraps," said Amanda. "I wonder if they serve that with mashed turnip and boiled potatoes?"

"Here's our waitress, you can ask her."

Their orders made to their satisfaction, they relaxed with a cup of coffee to wait for their meals. The candle on the table cast a soft flickering glow around them seeming to enclose them in their own private world. The sea breeze sighed around the window, and little bobbing lights on the harbour marked the return of the fishing boats from their day's labours on the water.

"So what frightened you in the attic today?" asked Alec.

"My imagination, I think. It can be very active, as you well know."

"But you always temper it with common sense," he protested. "I've never seen you so pale and nervous before. What was wrong?"

Amanda shrugged. "It's really nothing. The house's old and creaky, and the attic's shadowy. That's all."

"I think it's more than that," said Alec. "You've never been so frightened before. You didn't see yourself when I came through the door. I thought you were going to scream."

She sighed. "I guess I was." She looked at him seriously for a moment. "You know I don't believe in ghosts, and you know how long Aunt Martha lived there, and how many times I've stayed with her and slept in that very maid's room, and played in the attic on rainy days when I was little." She paused for breath. "Well, the other day, when I was showing Trudy the house, we went up to the attic so I could show her our ideas for a playroom. She had Roderick with her, and he started talking about a pretty lady and ran toward the west end of the attic. When he got there, he looked around and said, 'pretty lady gone,' as if he was really disappointed."

Alec frowned. "Did you and Trudy see anything?"

"Neither one of us was looking. Anyway, it's pretty shadowy down there with only the one light bulb at the top of the stairs."

"Were you frightened then?"

"Not really. I don't believe in ghosts, so that wasn't a

problem for me. Trudy seemed pretty cool about the whole thing, too. She went down the attic after Roderick and brought him back. We more or less agreed that it was just shadows."

Alec sat quietly thinking for a few minutes. "How do you feel about ghosts now?"

"I still don't believe in them, if that's what you're asking." She poured them both more coffee. "However, it did rather startle me when young Roddy woke up from his nap saying that the pretty lady had been rocking him, and that she was crying. I thought he'd have forgotten her by then."

Alec pursed his lips. "And he hadn't."

"No, and it's kind of been on my mind all week why he hadn't. I think some people have the second sight, and his grandmother told fortunes. You remember Trudy's mother, don't you?"

"Old Agnes? Sure I do. Who could forget her? The kids were all scared of her. Don was the only one who would talk to her, but only if he had to, and only in the daytime. The rest of us would all run when we'd see her coming." Alec smiled wryly at the memory. "We weren't even very confident about Gertrude, you know."

"I remember. All of us girls were just horrible to her. I never really got to know her until nurses' training, and then only slightly. By that time she was so prickly and scared of relationships she didn't really know how to make friends. She's changed a lot since then."

"What made you invite her over?" asked Alec as their supper arrived.

Amanda opened her napkin and arranged her cutlery to her liking while she thought. "I don't know exactly. I met her uptown a few days before, and I guess I was lonely. Anyway we made a date for her to come and have tea and see the house, and she came. She's the first of any of my classmates I've seen since we came home. The rest have either moved off the Island, or haven't been in when I called, and I've been very busy getting the house in order too." She shrugged. "I don't really know."

"I think we need to expand our circle of friends," said Alec after some thought. "Not to exclude Trudy and Don, but just to dilute the influence a little. After all, Don was a good friend of mine in high school."

"He was?" said Amanda. "I always thought he was such a jock hockey player. How did you get to know him? You spent all your time in the library with your nose in a book."

"So did he, when he wasn't playing hockey. But no one knew that except me and Don and the librarian. He kept it pretty quiet. Even Carole didn't know, and she was his girlfriend."

Amanda scraped up the last bite of potato from her plate. "How'd he arrange that?"

"He was on real good terms with Mrs. Beck, she was still the librarian then, and she used to let him sit in that little alcove behind her desk and read. No one could see him there. He'd spend hours in there reading psychology and studying."

"How'd you find out?"

"I caught him coming out of there one day." Alec laughed at the memory. "Boy, was he embarrassed! He swore me to secrecy, and told me that if I ever told anyone, he'd beat up on me. I looked at him, and then I looked at me, and I decided right then that he could have his own way."

Amanda laughed. "He was pretty big in those days wasn't he."

"He still is. I saw him at a distance downtown the other day, and he hasn't changed much in ten years. You said they have a child?"

"Yes, the precocious Roderick. He's a cute little fellow, full of gab, and hears and understands everything. Gertrude already has to spell things in front of him. He's got her red hair and blue eyes, but I think he's going to be big like his father."

"I wonder what kind of father Don makes? He always said he wanted lots of children."

"I guess he's good at being a family man. Trudy seems very happy." Amanda sat back as the waitress came to clear their plates. They made their dessert orders.

Alec poured more coffee, then sat back in his chair. "I wonder what kind of father I'll make?" he mused. "Now that you have the house just about the way you want it, we need to start thinking about our main reason for returning home." He smiled at Amanda.

She sighed. "I know. It's been on my mind a lot lately. I'm not getting any younger, and if we don't reproduce soon, we might as well forget it." She sat lost in thought for a few minutes. "I really do want a little Alec and Amanda," she added.

"I'll do my best," said Alec, as the dessert came. "Eat up

and we can go home and begin practising."

They drove home in a companionable silence, Amanda's small hand resting comfortably on Alec's thigh.

Much later that night Amanda surfaced from a heavy sleep. A thin cry seemed to echo through the thick darkness of the early morning.

"Alec! Wake up! I thought I heard a baby crying." She poked the sleeping Alec hard in the ribs.

"'S just cats," muttered Alec and went back to sleep.

CHAPTER 3

Don sat at the kitchen table reading yesterday's issue of the Guardian. I never seem to have time to keep up with this, he thought. I'm always a day behind. He gradually became aware of Gertrude talking to him from the the other side of the table. He frowned in an effort to recall what she'd said a moment ago. "What's that you said?" He set down the paper.

Gertrude laughed. "I knew you weren't listening. I had this feeling of talking to the proverbial wall. Quite unlike you, my dear." She poured herself a second cup of tea then lifted the pot in his direction.

He shook his head. "I'm sorry. I'm listening now." He reached across the table and patted her hand.

"I said, I think we should invite Amanda and Alec over for supper tomorrow night."

"Kind of short notice, isn't it?"

"Mm, maybe. I don't think they've met up with very many old friends since they've come back. Amanda's been busy with the house and all. Anyway, they can always refuse."

"No harm in asking, I suppose," said Don, folding up the newspaper. "I have to get going. I have that early appointment today. I'll be glad when she decides she doesn't need me anymore."

"Or at least needs you at a more reasonable hour, eh?"

"That would do too," said Don leaning over Gertrude. "Give us a kiss, and I'll see you this afternoon." He left by the back door slamming it behind himself.

Roderick appeared in the doorway in rumpled pyjamas. "Daddy gone?" he asked, rubbing the sleep from his eyes with a small fist and yawning hugely.

"You just missed him, sleepy head." Gertrude picked him up for a hug. "What d'you want for breakfast, toast and egg, or cereal?" She set him down at his place at the table.

"Toast and peanut butter," said Roderick.

"You got it," said Gertrude as she put two slices of bread

in the toaster and pushed the lever. "Would you like to have Mrs. MacIntyre over for supper some day?"

"Can the pretty lady come too?" asked Roderick.

Gertrude looked sharply at her son. I thought he'd forgotten about that by now, she thought. "Honey, there is no pretty lady. That was just shadows from the trees outside that you saw."

"But she talks to me," said Roderick. "So she must be real."

The toast popped, and Gertrude reached for a plate. What am I going to tell him to convince him that there is no pretty lady? she thought. "When does she talk to you?"

"Every night before I go to sleep."

Gertrude sighed with relief. "Just like Paulie," she pointed out.

"Yes, except Paulie's inside my head and plays with me whenever I want him to, and the pretty lady is outside my head and only comes at night when she wants to."

Gertrude groaned to herself. What is this child seeing? she wondered. Don thought it was bad enough when he discovered that I could see things that weren't there for most people, what'll he do when he finds out about this?

I need to talk to Mary Ann. To Roderick she said, "I see. What does the pretty lady look like?"

"She has long hair and always wears a nightie."

"One like mine?" asked Gertrude setting the plate of toast and peanut butter in front of her son.

"No-o, not like yours." Roderick thought hard for a minute. "D'you remember the picture of the old lady with the candle out at Uncle Jim's? Well, it's like that."

Gertrude remembered it well, a thick all-enveloping garment of a century ago. A high neck and long sleeves were the height of its fashion.

"What does she say to you when she talks to you?"

"She calls me her baby and strokes my hair. Sometimes she sings to me."

"You're not afraid of her?" Gertrude poured herself another cup of tea and sat down at the table across from Roderick.

"No-o!" replied Roderick in little boy scorn. "She's nice to me."

"Honey, not everyone who's nice to you is necessarily a good friend to have." Gertrude wracked her brains for a way of telling Roderick to be careful of strangers without scaring him to death.

"Why not?" asked the ever reasonable Roddy.

Gertrude sighed. "Because there're a few people out there who're nice to people just to get them to do bad things. That's why you have to be careful not to be too friendly with strangers. If they need help, help them, but don't get in cars with them, or go into houses with people you don't know."

"What if they might be a good friend to have?"

"You don't know that. Sometimes even big people can't tell who's a good friend to have."

"What about the pretty lady? She's not really here, you know."

"I know, honey, so there's not much I can do about her. She's not the kind of person who can hurt you anyway." I hope, thought Gertrude. "What d'you say we go to the park this morning?"

"Oh, boy!" shouted Roderick. "Can I play on the big guns?"

"Of course you may, but finish your toast first. You'll need lots of energy to play pirates."

❖

The day was soft with a faint promise of summer in the gentle breeze that blew in from the Strait. Spring flowers bloomed in the gardens around Beaconsfield, their brightness a joy to see after the long, cold maritime winter. Their steps took them past Government Pond and the Lieutenant Governor's mansion, and into Victoria Park. Roderick ran to and fro on the greening grass shrieking his delight at being outdoors. Gertrude pushed the empty stroller and enjoyed the spring day. Charlottetown harbour glistened in the morning sunlight, the soil along its edge still darkly red from the brief dawn shower.

"I'll race you to the first cannon," challenged Gertrude.

"Ready, set, go!" yelled Roderick, and ran giggling toward the goal.

Gertrude pretended to hurry after him.

"I won! I won!" shouted Roderick. "I ran the fastest!"

"You did indeed." Gertrude laughed down at Roderick's glowing face. "What are you going to pretend today?"

Roderick thought for a moment. "I'm going to pretend that I'm watching for the boat from Boston." He climbed up on the nearest cannon and straddled the barrel. Even though the sun was behind him, he put his hand up to his forehead to shade his eyes and looked out to sea. A lone seagull swooped and floated on the updraughts over the harbour. Gertrude sat down on the bench nearby and watched over him as he played.

Presently he returned to Gertrude's side and leaned against her knees looking up at her. "Mommy, I don't like that man." He pressed hard against her knees.

"What man, dear?" Gertrude looked around and saw no one.

"That man over there with the funny hat." He pointed toward the farthest cannon.

Gertrude looked where Roderick was pointing, but no one was there. "Are you sure you saw someone?"

"He talked to me, but he's gone now." Roderick sighed. "Is that what you meant when you said about good friends and bad friends, Mommy?"

Gertrude nodded. "That is what I meant."

"Can we go home now, please?"

"Already? We just got here."

Roderick climbed up on the bench beside her, and stared listlessly out to sea. Gertrude felt his forehead. It was cool. "Are you not feeling well, Roddy?"

"That man. It doesn't feel good down here today. I want to go home."

"Okay, we'll go right now. Do you want to ride in the stroller?"

"Yes, please." Roderick slid down off the bench and climbed into the stroller. Gertrude strapped him in and pushed off toward the entrance. I wonder what's gotten into him today, she thought. He always loves to play down here... I wonder who the mysterious man with the funny hat was? I certainly didn't see anyone, at least not in the physical... Oh dear, I wonder if he's going to be a psychic like me? I hope not. I hope so. Oh, I don't know what I want for him. Don won't be happy about this. Oh, dear. She walked along briskly. I guess I'll just have to keep a psychic watch on him too, at least until he's big enough to understand and look out for himself.

Presently Roderick began to sing to himself, "Pretty lady, pretty lady."

Gertrude hummed to herself as she waited for the directory assistance operator to answer. We haven't had anyone in for supper since before Christmas, she thought. I do hope they can come. Obtaining the MacIntyres' number from the operator, she dialled and waited. Amanda answered the phone on the first ring.

"Amanda? That was quick. You must have been right there, eh?"

"Is that you, Gertrude?"

"Yes, I was wondering if you and Alec were free for dinner tomorrow night. We'd certainly enjoy spending the evening with you."

"I'll need to check with Alec and get back to you. Will that be all right? He's working late this evening. He had a meeting to go to. Can I call you in the morning?"

"That'll be fine. Just give me time enough to fix the roast."

"Well, I'll talk to you in the morning then. About nine?"

"I'll wait for you. Good-bye, then."

Gertrude replaced her receiver. I wonder if I perceived a little reluctance in Amanda, she thought. She shook her head dismissively, I'm just imagining things. She wandered into the living room where Don sat reading the Guardian. Yesterday's Guardian lay in a crumpled heap at his feet. Gertrude bent to pick it up.

Don set the paper aside and reached out, pulling her

onto his lap. "So what did she say?" He snuggled her into the crook of his arm.

"Alec wasn't home. She wanted to check with him. She'll call me in the morning."

"I see." Don was silent for a moment. "Do I detect a little of the old suspicion in your tone of voice?"

Gertrude looked away. "I'm trying not to, but the tone of voice was there, and the reluctance to commit." Tears welled up in Gertrude's blue eyes. "It's times like this that I could really dislike my mother. Why did she have to act like such a crazy?" She sniffed back a sob.

Don cuddled her closer and stroked her hair. "I don't know, honey. I didn't know your mom very well."

Gertrude laughed wryly and sniffed again. "But you're the psychologist!"

"Not when I was acquainted with your mother," he said. "I was just as scared of her as the other kids were, I just wasn't going to give in and run like they did."

"Brave boy!" said Gertrude.

Don shrugged. "Not brave, just stubborn."

The telephone rang and Gertrude got up to answer it. It was Amanda.

"Alec got home just after you called. We'll be pleased to come to supper. What time?"

"About seven will be good. I'll have Roderick ready for bed. He can say hello and then go right upstairs. That way we can have an adult evening without little ears taking in everything and making comments."

Amanda chuckled. "I guess it must get a little wearying after a whole day of keeping up with him."

"I love him dearly, but I'm sometimes glad when he goes to bed."

"But I'll bet it's always good to see him again in the morning," said Amanda. "I'm sure looking forward to having my own."

"Speaking of which, I must go and check on him. I can hear him talking to himself up there, and it's time he was asleep."

"So seven o'clock tomorrow evening. We're looking forward to it. Good-bye then."

Gertrude replaced the receiver and stopped in the living room door on her way upstairs. "I guess I was just being silly." She smiled at Don. "They seem quite pleased to come."

She started up the stairs. Roderick's voice chattered on in conversational cadences with pauses every now and then as if he were talking to someone. Gertrude peeked around the edge of his door and listened for a moment. "Who're you talking to, honey?" She flipped on the light and glanced toward the foot of the bed. A white form was dissolving into the shadows at the edge of the room. She swept the small narrow room with her eyes, taking in the blue and green pirate ship wallpaper with the crossed swords border. The navy blue curtains moved slightly in a draft. She pulled them aside to check the window and the space created by the draperies.

"Pretty lady," replied Roderick. "She visits me every night now."

"She does?" asked Gertrude in alarm. "Where does she sit when she talks to you?"

"On the foot of my bed. She tells the nicest stories."

"Is she nicer than Paulie?"

Roderick thought for a moment. "No-o," he said slowly, "but Paulie isn't like she is. Paulie's just inside my head."

"Is she still here?"

"Not now. She left when you turned on the light. Didn't

you see her?"

"Not properly. Do you know what her name is?"

"She told me once. It's a funny name. Pooh something. I can't say it, so I just call her pretty lady. I want to go to sleep now, Mommy."

"Okay, darling, I'll just tuck you in again." Gertrude bent to pull up the blankets. "I don't want you to go anywhere with pretty lady," she said as she leaned over to kiss him goodnight for the second time.

"Oh, Mommy, of course not. I can't go with her. She lives somewhere else and I can't go there." He was silent for a moment. "Besides, I want to stay here with you and Daddy." He snuggled farther under the blankets. "Goodnight, Mommy," he yawned.

"Goodnight, Roddy, sleep tight, don't let the bedbugs bite." Gertrude turned out the light and closed the door over. Now what am I going to do about that? she wondered. At least he knows he can't go with her. I wonder who she is—was?

CHAPTER 4

Saturday dawned bright and beautiful. The sunlight still had its morning radiance about it when Gertrude belted Roderick into his car seat and set off for the grocery store in the mall. Traffic was light as they drove out University Avenue. "There's where you'll be going to school someday, Roderick," she said as they passed the University of Prince Edward Island.

"Pretty lady, pretty lady," sang Roderick to himself.

"Is the pretty lady with us now?" asked Gertrude.

"No," replied Roderick, "I was just thinking about her. Can I stay up and see Mrs. 'Tyre tonight, Mommy?"

"You may stay up and greet her and Mr. MacIntyre,

then you must go to bed. Tonight's just for big people. Besides, you need to get a good sleep tonight, tomorrow's Sunday school.

"Oh, boy," said Roderick, "I like to go to Sunday school." He subsided into happy humming again.

Gertrude turned into the parking lot and, after a lot of searching, found a parking space. "There's a crowd here today so this is kind of far from the door, Roddy, we'll have to walk."

"Walking's good for us," he said.

Gertrude laughed. "How d'you know that?"

"Big Bird said so."

"Well, if Big Bird said so, I guess it must be true. I wish I'd brought your stroller though." They set off across the parking lot.

They entered the mall and discovered a large crowd of people gathered in the middle. "Oh, look, Roderick, a petting zoo. D'you want to go and pat the animals?"

Roderick let go of Gertrude's hand, shot across the intervening space and burrowed his way through the crowd to the fence corralling the animals. "Look, Mommy, look, I'm patting a sheep," he called. "Ooh, soft." The sheep nuzzled the palm of his hand for the salty taste of his perspiration.

Gertrude let him pat for a few minutes, then called him. "One more minute, please, Mommy," he begged. "The sheep is talking to me." Gertrude rolled her eyes. "He has a great imagination," she said to the woman standing beside her.

In a few minutes Roderick returned. "That sheep is not happy here," he said loudly. "She wants to go home. Can we take her home, Mommy?"

"No, honey, we don't know where she lives. Besides she's probably going home this evening."

Roderick darted back toward the sheep. "My mommy says you're going to go home tonight," he said. He patted the sheep gently on the nose one more time, then ran back to Gertrude. "She's happier now, Mommy."

"That's good," said Gertrude. "C'mon now, we have to get groceries and get home again. I have to make a dessert for this evening, and Daddy'll be missing us." She took him by the hand and headed off to get a basket. "Up you go," she said, hoisting Roderick into the seat. "Now you can see everything."

"I think I'll roast a chicken for this evening," she said. She rooted through the bulk vegetables for carrots and a turnip. "I'll just make an old-fashioned chicken dinner. Your daddy likes that and it makes a good company meal."

"It's always good for leftovers too," said Roderick.

Gertrude laughed. "Where'd you hear a big word like leftovers?"

"I heard you say it to Aunt Mary Ann that day we had supper out at Uncle Jim's. You were talking about what to put in hash."

"Where were you?"

"I was playing with my truck on the floor."

"And you knew what we were saying?"

"Well, I'm not stupid, you know!" Roderick regarded his mother with his serious, bright blue gaze. "I'm almost four."

Gertrude shook her head. "That you are, and I can see I'm going to have to guard my conversations with you around. It's a good job you're going to bed when our guests get here tonight."

❖

Promptly at seven the doorbell rang. "Right on time." Gertrude greeted her guests.

Amanda laughed. "It's the nurses' training. Even though I'm not working at it anymore, I still don't dare be late for anything."

"I remember," said Gertrude. "It was sometimes the bane of my existence as a student. I think I was punished for that more often than any of the other girls. C'mon in, supper's just about ready."

"And it sure smells good," said Alec. He shook hands with Don. "Nice to see you again. It's been a long time."

"Ten years or so, isn't it?" Don led the way into the living room.

"Twelve, I think. At least that's what it feels like."

"Make yourselves comfortable, folks, I'll have supper on the table in a jiffy," said Gertrude.

"And who's this young man?" asked Alec, as Roderick slipped into the room and stood by the door sucking his finger.

"This is our son, Roderick, playing a little shy this evening, I think. Say good evening to Mr. MacIntyre, Roderick."

Roderick came forward and shook hands damply with Alec. "Good evening Mr. 'Tyre. I was at your house the other day. Does the pretty lady still live there?"

Alec looked startled. "What pretty lady is this, Roderick? The only pretty lady who lives at my house is Mrs. MacIntyre."

Roderick looked confused. "You know, the one who lives in the play room upstairs."

"There's no one who lives in the play room at my house, Roderick. The play room is empty. There's not even any furniture in it yet."

"But I saw her," protested Roderick. "And she comes to visit me here every night before I go to sleep."

"That's enough, Roderick," said Don. "If Mr. MacIntyre says there's no one living in his attic, then he should know, and you shouldn't question him about it. It's not polite. Now say good-night, and I'll come and tuck you in."

"But I did see her," said Roderick softly to himself as he turned to go.

"Roderick!" said Don, "no back talk."

"Was talking to myself," said Roderick under his breath as he climbed the stairs.

❖

"Supper's on the table," said Gertrude. "Where's Don?"

"He just took Roderick up to bed," said Amanda.

Presently Don joined them in the large dining room where the chandelier gave a glow as soft as candle light to the pale yellow walls. Even the maroon curtains seemed to glow. Family photos from olden times accented the walls and a low bouquet of orange and yellow flowers graced the delicate lace of the table cloth set with Getrude's fine china and her grandmother's silverware.

Don shook his head. "That kid's turning into a real case. He's up there insisting that the pretty lady is real, and that she visits him every night before he goes to sleep."

"He's got quite the imagination." Alec laughed. "That's a good thing though, it'll fill many childhood hours with enjoyment."

Gertrude and Amanda exchanged glances that said to each other, 'but you weren't there, Alec.'

"Well, sit in everyone. I'll stay here by the door so I can get back and forth to the kitchen easily, the rest of the places are yours for the choosing." She took her place at the end of the oval oak table, and Don sat down beside her. "We always give a blessing before we eat. Don?"

Everyone bowed their heads. "Dear Lord," intoned Don, "Thank you for this food and good friends to share it with. May it contribute to our physical and spiritual growth, in Jesus' name, amen."

"Well, now, everyone, dig in. Don, you start the potatoes, Alec, help yourself to the chicken. Amanda, perhaps you'll start the vegetables."

"So, Alec, Amanda tells me you're head of the Social Services," said Don. "That's a good position to have. It went empty for quite awhile before they found you."

"Yes, and there was quite a backlog of work when I got there, too. I'm just now getting out from under it." Alec helped himself to a chicken leg and thigh.

"He's been working late almost every evening since we got home," said Amanda. She helped herself to potatoes.

"That must make it kind of lonely for you." Gertrude took the bowl of mashed potatoes from her.

"It has been lately. I've nearly finished the house-cleaning and painting. I still want to paper that little room that I showed you at the top of the stairs, but it seems almost a little precipitate since we want to use it for the nursery and I'm not even pregnant yet. I'm afraid it'll jinx our plans." She laughed, embarrassed by her admission of superstition. "I know I'm being silly, but I can't help it."

Gertrude remembered the shiver of uneasiness that had crawled down her spine as she stood on the stairs leading from that room to the attic. "Perhaps you're right," she said. "I never did believe in tempting fate myself."

Silence came over the dining room, punctuated by the chink of silverware on good china, as they all turned their attention to their meal: moist chicken accompanied by fluffy, mashed, Island potatoes, carrots, and yellow turnip, all covered over with rich chicken gravy.

"Seconds, anyone?" offered Gertrude after a few minutes. "Be sure to leave room for dessert."

"I've had plenty, thanks," said Alec wiping up the last of his potatoes and gravy with his last bite of chicken.

"That was delicious," said Amanda, wiping her fingers on her napkin. "It's been ages since I've had such a feast."

"I'll just go and make the tea then." She rose from her place. "Pass me your plates, and I'll only need to make the one trip."

She returned presently with a tea pot warmer. "Plug that in behind you, will you, please, Don? I got this in the States when I was down for Mom's funeral. It's actually for a coffee pot, but it's the greatest rig for keeping the tea warm too." She returned to the kitchen and came back in with a plate of cheese. "It's our own Island cheese," she said, "it's good and buttery. I have some apple pie to go with it."

"So what do you do in your spare time?" asked Alec, taking a bite of flaky pie crust and sweet apples.

"What spare time?" Gertrude laughed. "I work as an assistant to a researcher. I do a variety of things."

"Jill of all trades, eh? What kind of research?"

Gertrude hesitated. In for a penny, in for a pound, she thought. "He investigates paranormal occurrences," she said, and held her breath waiting for their reaction.

"Oh," said Alec. He was momentarily at a loss for words. Then: "Anyone we know?"

"No," said Don. "He's a Nova Scotian. I met him at Dalhousie when I was working on my Master's. We became good friends, and I went on a couple of research trips with him when we were students. He worked for the Canadian Society for Paranormal Research when he was a student, and did such a good job, they asked him to come on full time when he graduated. He has his PhD. in psychology too. He's a researcher though."

"A Bluenoser, eh? How'd he get to the Island?"

"He worked in Toronto for awhile after he graduated, but he always wanted to come home. There was enough work in the Maritimes so the Society allowed him to work here, and report there, which suited him right down to the ground. It only took him two weeks to get himself moved, he was that anxious to get home."

"Why'd he move to the Island?"

"His family was from here. He spent his summers here when he was growing up and always wanted to live here."

"And what do you do for him?" asked Amanda.

"A variety of things," replied Gertrude. "I keep his books in order, type up his notes, keep him generally organized. Things like that."

"Do you ever go out on cases with him?"

"I have been," said Gertrude. "My upbringing has rather suited me to dealing with the paranormal in a calmer manner than most people can."

"Oh, yes, your mother read fortunes, didn't she,"

said Alec.

Gertrude sighed. "Yes, unfortunately. She tried to make me learn how, but I rebelled. I hated the way we had to live with everyone afraid of us."

Amanda reached over and patted her hand. "Well, you don't have to live that way anymore."

Little do you know, thought Gertrude. I wonder how long we'd be friends if you knew that I was the principal psychic for our researcher? "Let's take our tea into the living room where it's more comfortable." She rose from her place at the table.

Talk turned to reminiscences as the evening wore on. Gertrude had little to say. She had never been a part of the group as a child, and so had no experiences in common with the others. I'm so thankful for Don and Roderick, she thought, but I feel so left out, even now, when they talk about the past. I wish so much that things had been different.

At home that night as they lay in the dark chatting about the evening, Alec said, "Did you get the impression that

Gertrude was hiding something about her job?"

"Mm, maybe. I thought she just didn't want to bring up the past. You notice that she had nothing to say for the rest of the evening."

"I guess you're right." Alec's voice trailed away into a gentle snore.

Amanda turned on her side to face the window, and soon drifted off. At three o'clock in the morning, just as the night was darkest, she came very wide awake, listening acutely as the cry of a baby in distress faded from her wakeful ears.

CHAPTER 5

On Tuesday, Amanda awakened to the sound of rain hammering on the roof and gushing through the downspout at the corner of her bedroom. A gloomy day, she thought. Just what I need with Alec going away for three days. I hope it doesn't last. She rolled out of bed and padded barefoot to the bathroom. In a few minutes she made her way downstairs to put the kettle on and start breakfast.

She recalled their conversation of the night before. It had almost turned into an argument. Alec had come home from work and announced that he had a meeting in Halifax on Wednesday and Thursday morning and wouldn't be back until Thursday evening. She had asked to go with him but he had refused, saying that she'd be bored with nothing to do while he was in meetings all day and evening. "My motel is out in Rockingham and you'd have to take the bus to get anywhere," he'd said. "And you don't know anyone in Halifax, so you can't go visiting."

"But I know Mrs. MacLeod on Robie Street," she'd protested. "She'd be happy to see me."

"Well you can't stay with her for two days, you'd wear out your welcome. Besides, don't you have a doctor's appointment tomorrow?"

"Please, Alec." She'd been almost in tears.

Alec pulled her into his arms. "What's the matter with you, Amanda? I've never seen you like this before."

With great effort Amanda had swallowed her distress and managed to smile and return his hug. "I'm sorry, Alec, I'm just being silly," she'd replied. I can't tell him that I'm scared to stay alone in this house at night, she thought.

The electric kettle came to a boil drawing Amanda back to the present. She poured water on the tea bags and set the pot on the burner at low to steep. Two fat brown eggs came to a boil on the front burner and Amanda pushed down the toast in the toaster. Three minute eggs and three minute toast, very convenient, she thought.

Alec came into the kitchen whistling. "A dismal day today," he said, buttoning his shirt sleeves and giving Amanda a peck on the cheek. "How're you feeling this morning?"

I still want to go with you, she thought, but I'm not asking again. "I'm okay," she said. The toast popped. She pulled it from the toaster and buttered it. "I guess I was just being silly." She pulled the eggs from the hot water with tongs, and set them deftly in the egg cups.

"What time are you leaving?" She set the food on the table.

"About eleven, I guess. I'm driving, so I have to be sure and be there on time to catch an early ferry. I heard yesterday that traffic is real heavy at both boats. Some people were waiting for two ferries before they could get on."

She poured the tea. "Which way're you going?"

"I thought Wood Islands. It's quicker once you get to the mainland."

They ate in silence for a few minutes. "If you get lonely, you can give Gertrude a call," said Alec. He sipped his tea.

"I suppose so. If she's free. Anyway, I've got that appointment this afternoon. That'll probably take up most of the afternoon."

"It probably will," said Alec. "Keep busy and the days won't seem so long."

It's not the days I'm worried about, thought Amanda. I can't tell him about the baby crying, he'll think I'm crazy. But it's been every night now for the past week. Maybe I am crazy. "I can always try calling some of my other friends again," she said. "P'raps I'll have better luck this time."

Alec finished his tea and pushed back from the table. "Do you want me to come back home before I leave?"

Amanda shook her head. "It's not necessary. I'll be all right."

"I put gas in the little car for you and checked the oil and the tires." He straightened his tie in the kitchen mirror. "Everything's shipshape, so you shouldn't have any trouble." He shrugged into his suit jacket. "Here's the number of the motel I'll be at, and the number of the place where the meetings are, if you need me for anything. C'mon and walk me to the door." He put an arm around her shoulders and together they walked to the front door. He turned her around to face him. "Now don't worry about anything, everything'll be just fine." He pulled her into a brief hug. "Just lock the doors behind yourself, I've already checked all the windows. You'll be quite safe. You know nothing ever happens on the Island." He picked up his suitcase, gave her another kiss, and was gone.

That's what you think, she thought. She closed the door behind him.

Her appointment with the doctor that afternoon confirmed her suspicions. I'm pregnant, she thought as she drove toward home. I wonder if I'll have a boy or a girl. Alec'll be so happy. I'm so happy! She hummed a tune as her little car splashed through the red puddles. It was still raining. I wish Alec was here. We could have celebrated this evening. I'll have to wait until he gets home. She pulled to a stop in her driveway and shut off the engine. That's what he gets for leaving me home, he'll just have to wait to hear the news. She squelched through the mud to the back door. I'm sure glad we have a porch. She bent to take off her rubbers. As she straightened, her glance fell over the backyard. A mist seemed to have gathered itself in the back corner. Oh, no, there's a fog coming in. I hate foggy nights by myself.

She closed and locked the door behind herself, then went into the kitchen and put the kettle on. I hope Alec didn't have a hard drive to Halifax. It was probably foggy over Mount Thom too, she thought. She made herself some tea, and carried it into the living room. Turning on the television set she flipped through the channels. Big money for cable and all you can get is cartoons, she thought, and shut the set off again. She sipped her tea. It's cold in here. I guess maybe I should put a little heat on. She went out to the hallway and turned up the thermostat. A cry seemed to fill the air. Amanda felt her hair stand on end.

"W-who's there?" There was no answer. I'm imagining things, she thought. The cry came again. "It sounds like it came from the cellar," she said aloud, the sound of her own voice a reassurance. She went into the kitchen, unhooked the cellar door and turned on the light. A half-grown black kitten sat on the top step. "Meow?" it said. It stretched itself and came into the kitchen.

"Well, Kitty, is it you who's been scaring me half to death every night? I'll bet you're hungry." She opened a can of tuna, spooned some of it into a saucer and set the dish on the floor. The cry came again. The cat's fur stood up on its back. It snarled and scurried under the stove.

Amanda dropped her tea cup. It smashed on the tile floor into five pieces and some crumbs. The remains of her tea splashed everywhere. "Oh, dear, Kitty, I guess it wasn't you after all." She gathered up the pieces with trembling fingers. "I wish Alec was here." The cat slinked out from beneath the wood stove. It kept a wary eye on its surroundings and began to gobble the tuna.

Amanda mopped up the tea. "It's getting dark out, Kitty. I guess you'd better stay the night. It's raining pretty hard out there. I hope you don't have fleas."

She began to fix herself some supper. Leftovers go good on a rainy night. I'll watch the news while I eat, she thought. She set her plate on a tray. She spooned some Lady Ross relish onto her plate beside the hash. She took down another mug from the cupboard and filled it with tea. It's strong enough to float a potato, but it'll have to do, she thought. Waste not, want not.

She carried her tray across the darkening hallway. A brief flutter of white at the top of the stairs seemed to catch the corner of her eye. She turned her head to look. There was nothing there. Or was there? A faint glow seemed to gather itself by the window and then dissipate.

Amanda almost dropped her tray, then became angry. "If that's you, Aunt Martha, you should be wherever it is spirits go! This is not funny!" she shouted. The glow was no longer there. A gentle chuckle, that was nothing like Aunt Martha's hearty laugh, seemed to echo on the air.

Amanda flipped on the hall light with the corner of her tray. This light stays on all night, she thought, and I'm sleeping down here with the rest of the lights on. The cat jumped onto the sofa beside her and made itself comfortable. I'm glad I've got you for company, thought Amanda.

She awoke early the next morning after a very restless night. Her dreams had been filled with babies crying while she frantically looked for them, but never seemed to find them.

"Good morning, Kitty," she said. "I hope you had a better night than I did."

Kitty yawned and stretched, then padded softly over to the door and sat down. "Meow?" said Kitty.

"D'you want to go out? I guess it's about time." Amanda eased herself off the couch and went to open the front door. "You'll be back for breakfast?"

Kitty rubbed around Amanda's ankles and purred, then went out onto the porch and sat down on the top step surveying the newly washed Island morning. A breeze, fresh from the Strait, carried the scent of the sea over the city. A faint odour of paper mill from Nova Scotia edged its saltiness. The rain had turned the pink Island sand to dark red mud, and red puddles lay everywhere. The day was as bright as a new copper penny.

Amanda watched Kitty as she made her way down the steps and out the front walk, stepping daintily between the puddles. "Come back anytime," she called softly after the departing cat. Now I must brave the upstairs, she thought, closing the door behind her. Might as well do it all at once. She took a deep breath and ran lightly up the stairs. I won't be able to do that for very many more months.

The upstairs was awash with morning sunlight, the stained glass window at the head of the stairs made soft patches of colour on the hardwood floor of the landing. "Now what's this doing here?" Amanda stooped to pick up the white bureau scarf and return it to its proper place on the hall table. That cat probably made free of the house last night. I hope it didn't leave any little presents around, it wasn't very eager to go out this morning, she thought.

A few minutes later she was showered and dressed and on her way down to the kitchen. I think I will call Gertrude this morning. Maybe she can spend some time with me today. She plugged in the kettle. This evening'll be a good time if she's free. She can get Don to stay with Roderick, and we can have a good visit. She poured cereal into a bowl. It'll be nice to have company for awhile.

Gertrude rang the door bell at Amanda's house at eight o'clock that evening. Amanda answered promptly. "Hi, Trudy, I'm so glad you could come over." She led the way into the living room. "We'll make ourselves comfortable in here. I just put the kettle on. I had a feeling you'd not be able to get away right when you thought you could. Don didn't mind babysitting, did he?"

"No, he and Roderick have a great relationship. They talk about everything under the sun."

"Your Roderick's an interesting little fellow, isn't he."

"A little too interesting sometimes, I think." Gertrude chuckled. "He still hasn't forgotten about the 'pretty lady' over here. He wanted to come tonight to see her again. He thinks that she lives here. His reasoning was that she visits him every night before he goes to sleep, so now it was time to return the visits. I had a hard time convincing him to stay home. That's why I was late."

Amanda shook her head. "She visits him? That's quite an imagination, and he's only three yet?"

"He's really almost four, but sometimes you'd think he was ninety-four, the things he comes up with, and all of it so logical."

"Excuse me for a minute, that kettle must be about boiled dry by now. I'll be back in a jiffy." Amanda disappeared toward the kitchen.

Gertrude made herself comfortable on the chesterfield and reflected on her son's precociousness. I wonder if it'll last?

she thought. Mary Ann seemed to think it will. She mulled over her visit with her friend on the previous evening. Don thought I was crazy to be going visiting in all that rain, but I needed to talk to Mary Ann. I hadn't seen her in such a long time, almost two weeks, and I needed to talk to her about Roderick.

She thought about the messy comfort of Mary Ann's kitchen with its wood stove that seemed to be perpetually smoking. The memory of the red geraniums on the window sill between the dusty curtains that hung askew made Gertrude smile. The grandmother clock on the clock shelf was always out of time by several minutes and some of the hours no longer struck at all. Somewhere there was always a mother cat with a few kittens in various stages of growth depending on the time of year. They were usually behind the stove.

"I think Roderick's got the gift," Gertrude said when they had settled themselves comfortably at the table over tea and chocolate chip cookies.

"I know." Mary Ann offered Gertrude the first cookie.

"You knew about it?"

"Molly told me when he was born."

"Why didn't she tell me? After all, I am his mother."

"You know Molly." Mary Ann had shrugged. "She always has some reason. She didn't want me to tell you about it because she said that you'd be watching for it instead of letting it develop naturally. I don't even think she was supposed to tell me. I think she just let it slip." Mary Ann took a bite of her cookie. "Does Don know?"

Gertrude sighed. "No, and I don't know if I should tell him. He worried so when we were trying to decide whether or not I was psychic or just plain crazy, I'm afraid of how he'll take it when he finds out about Roddy."

"Why tell him? Why not just let him discover it on his own like you did?"

"I think it won't be very long before he does discover it for himself." She recounted the events of recent days.

"So you think your friend's house is haunted. Have you told Jim about it yet?"

"No, this's all come about since he's been away. I'm not even sure if Amanda realizes what's going on yet. She says she doesn't believe in ghosts."

"She'll be changing her mind about that pretty soon." Mary Ann chuckled. "Have you talked to Molly lately?"

"No, I haven't done any trance work since Jim left. I haven't needed to, and I assume she hasn't needed me either, or she would have called me."

"Without regard for anyone but herself, likely." Mary Ann helped herself to another cookie, which snapped in two before she could touch it. "I see she's here now, and she's heard what I said."

Gertrude slipped easily into trance and came face to face with Molly. "Eavesdropping again, Molly?"

"Talking about me behind my back, eh?" Molly's black eyes sparkled. "Thought I was still on vacation, did you?"

"Actually, until this evening, I hadn't been thinking about you at all," Gertrude replied. "Besides I wasn't the one who was talking behind your back."

"Humph! Out of sight out of mind, I suppose. Where's big Jim these days?"

"He went to a conference in Toronto, then he went home to visit his mother in Nova Scotia for a couple of weeks."

"Momma's boy perhaps?"

"Certainly not," Gertrude said. "His mother's very old, and speaking of mothers, why didn't you tell me that Roderick would be psychic?"

"Because you weren't supposed to know until the time came." Molly's tone had been short and sharp.

"But you told Mary Ann."

"Yes, well, she wormed it out of me." Molly squirmed on the clock shelf.

"You mean you let it slip."

"These things do happen." Molly wriggled again making the clockworks vibrate tinnily.

"Quite often where you're concerned it seems." Gertrude didn't given Molly an inch. "Are you 'allowed' to tell me who the man in the funny hat was at the park the other day?"

"I would if I knew myself." Molly refused to apologize for her error. "I wasn't there, so I don't know."

"What about the 'pretty lady' he met at Amanda's the other day?"

"I wasn't there either," she replied. "Look, if all you can do this evening is pick on me, I'm leaving." She faded from Gertrude's inner vision without even a good-bye.

"She was certainly in a mood tonight, wasn't she," Mary Ann had said when Gertrude returned her attention to the physical.

"Yeah, she doesn't like being caught out," Gertrude

replied. "Sometimes I just can't believe that Molly. Ever since I've known her at the nursing home she's been contrary and secretive. You could never get around her." Gertrude thought back to the days before Molly's death, before Gertrude herself knew that she too had the 'gift.' "She and Lucy harassed me something awful from the astral plane after they and Larry taught her to get out of her body and go travelling with them. Of course, I didn't have a clue what was going on I was in such deep denial because of my mother and was nearly scared out of my wits." Gertrude laughed. "When they got through with me I didn't have very many wits left to be scared out of. And poor Don ..."

Mary Ann raised an eyebrow. "Molly certainly can be a handful. I was listening just now and watching her squirm when you got after her about Roddy. She didn't like it one little bit."

"I didn't know you were there."

"I was just listening a little, I didn't really join you."

❖

Gertrude was recalled to the present by Amanda's return with a tea tray.

"Here, let me help you with that." Gertrude took the other side of the heavy tray.

"I made us some nibblies this afternoon, I hope they're fit to eat. I never made them before." She set up the teacups and poured the tea.

"They certainly smell good, if that's any indication." Gertrude helped herself to the first one. "Mm, just perfect! I'll be as fat as a little piggie if my friends keep feeding me like this." She laughed. "When's Alec due back?"

"Tomorrow afternoon sometime. He has meetings in the morning, so he probably won't be here until nearly supper time, what with the boats and all."

"So how've you been keeping yourself busy since he left?"

"I had company last night too," said Amanda. "Well, company of sorts, at least."

"Oh?" Gertrude looked at her friend over the rim of her tea cup.

"Yes, and it nearly scared me to death too."

"It?"

"Yes, a little black kitten. She got into the cellar some

way or other, and was sitting on the top step crying to be let in. She was hungry, and it was raining so hard out I didn't have the heart to put her outside, so I let her stay the night. She asked politely to go out this morning, and I haven't seen her since."

"You should get yourself a pet, they're wonderful company."

"I was hoping all day that Kitty might come back, but she hasn't appeared, so I guess she won't be back now. Anyway, Alec isn't too fussy about having animals in the house, him being a farm boy and all. More tea?"

"A little drop, please. Well, if your plans work out the way you want them to, you won't be needing a pet, anyway."

Amanda glowed.

"You're already expecting!"

Amanda nodded. The sound of a baby crying filled the house. She paled and jumped to her feet. "That must be Kitty again." She hurried out to the kitchen with Gertrude close behind her, and opened the cellar door. Kitty wasn't there. Amanda slumped into a kitchen chair, her heart racing. The crying began again.

"Has this been happening much?" asked Gertrude.

Amanda nodded. "Alec just says it's cats."

"He's heard it too, then?"

"Oh, yes. That night after we were over at your house for supper we heard it."

"D'you feel up to checking out the house with me? It may be just a prankster."

"That's probably all it is. There's no such thing as ghosts, and that Mr. Nicks wanted to buy this place after Aunt Martha died, and I wouldn't put anything past him."

"Oh, yes, Mr. Nicks. He was my landlord before Don and I got married. He'd get up to no good all right."

"C'mon then," said Amanda, "I'm more than a match for Mr. Nicks."

They made a tour of the house and found nothing amiss.

"Well," Amanda shrugged, "so much for that theory. Let's have some more tea." She led the way downstairs. "Go on in to the living room. I'll just boil the kettle again and make us a fresh pot."

Gertrude entered the living room and settled herself on the chesterfield. Presently Amanda returned with a fresh pot of tea.

"Is that Kitty?" asked Gertrude, nodding toward the

little black cat that had followed Amanda into the room.

Amanda turned to look. "Oh, you rascal! Where've you been hiding? Did you let her in?"

"Not me," said Gertrude. "I thought you did."

CHAPTER 6

Amanda lay in bed that night mulling over the events of the evening. Kitty lay beside her purring gently. She had discussed the situation with Kitty earlier, and together they had decided that no matter what, or who, was making the noise, they would not be frightened out of their beds for a second night. "Besides, that chesterfield's lumpy," said Amanda.

"Meow," agreed Kitty, and yawned a whiskered yawn.

The ocean breeze blew in off the harbour and whispered softly around the eaves. Amanda pulled the sheets up to her chin and closed her eyes. "I'll be glad when Alec gets home, Kitty. He'll be so excited to hear about the baby. He's wanted one for such a long time. I can't wait to tell him."

The breeze seemed to have penetrated the house. The curtains stirred faintly, and somewhere in the house a door slammed. Amanda sat straight up in bed clutching the sheet. The hair on her neck rose, her heart pounded. Kitty sat up and stretched, then turned around and curled into a ball with her tail over her nose. Amanda let out the breath she'd been holding. "There must be a window open somewhere, Kitty," she reassured herself.

She settled back on the pillow again, and stared into the darkness, straining her ears to listen. I don't know what I'm listening for, she thought. I wish Alec was here.

Soft footsteps seemed to be come up the stairs and enter the maid's room. "W-who's there?" quavered Amanda. "I've got a gun." Now why'd I say that? I haven't even got a telephone up here, she chided herself. Now they know I'm here, and all alone too. Too much American television!

The footsteps pattered softly around the little room, then came quietly down the hallway. The door to Amanda's room seemed to move slightly. It's just a draft, she thought. There's no one there.

A faint glow crept around the edges of the door. It's just a passing car. Amanda disregarded the fact that her bedroom was on the back of the house and away from traffic.

The sound of a baby in distress filled the room. Well, that's not a car! she thought. Kitty leaped to her feet hissing and spitting, a ferocious black ball of fluff.

The glow in the doorway increased. Amanda sat clutching the sheet to her chin, too terrified to move. The door moved slightly as if the draft had increased. We've got to get those windows fixed, thought Amanda through her terror. She stared at the door, her eyelids stretched to their limits. The glow gathered itself into a pale form and instantly disappeared. Kitty shrieked and disappeared under the bed. The room lay in darkness again.

It was some minutes before Amanda could move. She reached out a trembling hand to turn on the light. "I-it's okay, Kitty, you can come out now, I-I think we'll sleep downstairs tonight."

Kitty stuck her head cautiously out from underneath the dust ruffle, her whiskers festooned with dust bunnies. "Meow?" she asked.

"C-come here, Kitty, it's all right now."

Kitty leaped onto the bed and burrowed under the sheet beside Amanda's warm legs. Amanda began to laugh hysterically. "You should see yourself, you silly cat." Tears streamed down her cheeks. "Everything's covered except your tail." She laughed until she had no more strength left. I guess it's better than crying, she thought in the rational part of her mind.

The bedside lamp was still burning when Amanda awoke from her heavy, dreamless sleep the next morning. Kitty was curled into a tight ball next to her feet underneath the sheet. The early morning sun darted and dipped around the room as the slight draft from the window gently moved the blind.

"Alec'll be home today, Kitty," said Amanda. She hopped out of bed, her experience of the night before still lying in the recesses of her memory.

"Meow?" Kitty slithered out from under the sheet and landed with a thump on the floor.

"Oh, I forgot, you haven't met Alec yet." Amanda stuck her feet into her pink slippers. "You'll like him. He's a nice man. At least I think so."

She padded off to the bathroom, stopping to rummage in the linen cupboard for a towel. Kitty followed her. "D'you want a shower too?"

"Meow," said Kitty. She made herself comfortable on the toilet tank.

"Well, suit yourself," said Amanda as she turned on the taps and adjusted the water to her satisfaction. She pulled the shower knob and climbed in as the water rumbled up the old-fashioned shower spout. She gasped as the water struck her warm skin. Drat! I forgot that the first water is always freezing. She stood for a moment letting the water warm to skin temperature. She picked up the soap and began to lather her body. The water felt good. She hummed a little song under her breath. Soon I'll be scrubbing for two, she thought, looking down at the gentle curve of her belly, already not quite as flat as it used to be. Even my breasts are fuller. Having babies is an amazing business. Alec will be so happy.

A faint echo of a baby's cry echoed in her mind. She stopped humming and dropped the soap. It clattered slickly to the bottom of the tub. "I didn't hear that," she said. She picked up the soap. "I'm imagining things. It's my condition." The memory of last night's terror came flooding back. She quickly finished her shower and climbed out of the tub and dried herself. It will never do to be caught without my clothes on, she thought. Kitty rose from her place on the toilet tank and stretched. Her back arched and her paws spread, then she repeated the process in the opposite direction. Even her tail seemed to stretch.

"Did you you hear that, Kitty?" She tidied the bathroom hurriedly. "No, I can see you didn't, judging by your lack of distress."

Sticking her head out the bathroom door, she checked the hallway for signs of …? What am I checking for? she thought in annoyance. Certainly not ghosts. She marched back to her room with her chin high, the breeze of her passing making a cold spot on her back that she hadn't managed to dry in her haste. She dressed and made the bed. "From the look of your whiskers last night, I guess I'd better get out the mop one of these days," she said to Kitty.

Amanda heard Alec's key in the lock at noon. She ran to greet him. "I'm so glad to see you!" She threw her arms around Alec's skinny frame. "You're home early."

Alec held her tightly. "Are you okay?"

Amanda looked puzzled. "Of course I am. Why wouldn't I be?"

"Oh, no reason." Alec planted a kiss on her lips. "Have you had lunch?"

"Not yet, I was just thinking about it." Amanda broke from his embrace and led the way to the kitchen. "What would you like?"

"Whatever you're having." Alec hung his jacket behind the stove. "Anything exciting happen while I was away? How'd the doctor's visit go?"

"Fine."

"Well?"

Amanda smiled widely at him. "It's a baby!"

Alec pulled her into his arms with a joyous shout.

All was quiet in the kitchen for a few minutes as Alec stood rocking her gently in his arms. "That's wonderful!" he said at last. "When?"

"Early next year, he thinks." She slipped from his arms and began preparing lunch. "D'you have to go back to the office this afternoon?"

"They don't know I'm here yet, and I do have a lot of overtime that I'm not likely to get unless I take it. I guess I could just tell them I'm taking some."

"Why are you here so soon?" she asked as she set out the place mats.

Alec laughed. "You could say I missed you."

"But you wouldn't," said Amanda.

"Well, I did, but that's not the reason I came home early."

"So, why did you come home early?"

Alec pursed his lips. "I had a bad dream about you last night. It was very real and it made me uneasy."

Amanda set out cutlery and napkins. "What was it about?"

"I dreamed you were in danger here at the house. That the cats we keep hearing in the night are really babies in distress, and that you're the focus of their crying. Silly wasn't it!"

"Meow," agreed Kitty from her place of comfort under the stove.

Alec jumped. "Where'd that beast come from?"

Amanda laughed. "That's our new friend. She came the night of the rainstorm and decided to stay. By the way, you'll need to check in the cellar for ways in and out for beasties such as herself. I found her at the top of the cellar steps, and she was nice and dry, so she must have been there for some time."

"I'll do that," said Alec. "It's all very well to give shelter to one stray, but what if she tells her friends?"

Amanda set a plate of sandwiches on the table and poured the tea. "It's funny, you know, she seems to have a way into this part of the house as well. I put her out yesterday morning, and I didn't see her all day, and last night when Gertrude was here, she pranced into the living room as big as life, and neither of us had let her in."

"Hm, I guess I will have to check out the cellar." Alec helped himself to a sandwich. "So you had Gertrude over? What was her news?"

Amanda shrugged. "Nothing much, we just talked babies, and she helped me search the house."

"Search the house!" Alec spoke around a mouthful of chicken salad sandwich.

"Yes, we heard that cat crying, except it didn't sound like a cat."

"Where was Kitty then?"

"I don't know, she hadn't come in yet. Or if she had, she was upstairs."

"Did you find anything?"

"No, there was nothing amiss, and right after we came down I went to make some more tea, and when I brought it into the living room, Kitty appeared from somewhere and followed me in as if she owned the place. We decided that it must be someone up to pranks."

"Hallowe'en is months away," said Alec. "Did you hear the cats crying at all?"

Amanda hesitated and then recounted her experience of the night before. "But now that I think about it in the daylight, I think it must have been a dream. I was pretty tired last night, and now that I'm pregnant, dear knows what I'll be dreaming up."

"That must have been just about the time I was having my nightmare. I wanted to leave right then, but the boats weren't running so I had to wait. I left in time for the six o'clock boat, but of course there was a line. And what with all the big trucks, and it being almost tourist season, I didn't get on 'til nine."

"You came Wood Islands?"

"Yes, it's closer even if you have to wait and you never know what the wait'll be at Cape Tormentine either." Alec swallowed the last of his tea. "Well, I guess I'd better call the office and let them know I'm back. Then we'll check the house over for cat holes and other abnormalities."

He went out to the hall to make his call, and Amanda cleared the table. I hope we don't find any 'abnormalities,' she thought. I don't think I can take too many more of these 'abnormal' nights.

Alec returned after a minute or two. "Are you ready to go on the great search?"

Amanda sighed. "As ready as I'll ever be." She dried her hands on the towel.

They made their way upstairs. "I'll check the maid's room and the attic first," said Alec, "since that's where you heard the noise. You stand here in the doorway until I call you."

Alec made a thorough tour of the room and found nothing. He climbed the stairs to the attic turning on the light by its dangling string as he went. "There's nothing up here, either," he shouted after a few moments. "Just the boxes of books we put up here when we moved in. The dust hasn't even been disturbed." He clattered down the stairs. "You can go up and look if you want."

"No thanks, I'll believe you." Amanda shuddered. "Turn off the light and let's get on with this."

They searched the rest of the upstairs. In their bedroom Alec turned back the bed covers to reveal a small, cat-sized residue of black fur at the bottom of the bed. "So you didn't dream about her sleeping with you, at least."

"No, she was there in the morning. She didn't get out until after I did."

Alec got down on his knees and lifted the dust ruffle. "Hand me the flashlight, it's as dark as Egypt down here."

Amanda rummaged in the bedside table and found the flashlight. Now why didn't I think of this thing last night, she thought. She handed it to Alec.

"Well, Kitty was definitely under here some time or other, there are skid marks in the dust," said Alec.

They returned to the kitchen. Amanda made another pot of tea. "So what do we do now?"

"We wait," said Alec. "There's a rational explanation for everything. There was no sign of anyone having been here, so there probably wasn't anyone here. Kitty could have been under the bed any time besides last night."

"I guess it really was all a dream. We must be pretty close if my dreams can influence your dreams," she said.

"Meow," agreed Kitty from under the stove.

CHAPTER 7

"Time for bed, Roderick," called Gertrude from the kitchen. "Ask Daddy to help you pick up your toys." The sound of small truck engines continued from the living room. "Roderick!"

"Yes, Mommy?"

"You heard what I said."

"Daddy's not here."

Gertrude sighed. "Where is he, then?"

"He's in the den reading." Roderick continued with his play.

Gertrude went to the door of the den, a small book-lined room off the living room. "Don, can you help

Roderick pick up his toys while I finish in here, please? I have to get these sandwiches finished and into the fridge before I give everyone ptomaine poisoning."

Don followed her back to the kitchen. "All these for us?"

"No, they're for the church tea tomorrow. I promised to make two loaves." She began cutting off the crusts.

Don swiped them as they fell from the knife. "Which tea is this now?"

"The 'Spring into Summer' tea. I told you about it last week. The W.M.S. is putting it on." She wrapped the first bunch of uncut sandwiches in waxed paper and packed them into the bread bag. "It's a fund raiser for us."

"And what are you going to use the funds for?"

"Some of it's going to buy new drapery for the pulpit. I guess the rest will go for various other mission projects as it usually does. There'll be a craft table, too."

"Is that why you've been so diligently crocheting these last few weeks?"

"Yes, doilies are about all I can make on such short notice. I just hope everyone else doesn't bring them too."

"D'you need me to keep Roddy?"

"It'd be a big help, at least for part of the afternoon. I

have to serve. They're offering a day care, but you know him and day care."

Don laughed. "Yeah, he's a little too reasonable for the other three year olds, and too small yet to go with boys of his intellectual equal."

"If there are any," said Gertrude.

"Any what?" Roderick appeared in the doorway.

"Sandwiches," said Don. "Look at you! I guess you didn't need any help getting ready for bed."

Roderick looked down at himself. "I guess maybe I did." He tugged at his pyjama tops which were buttoned crooked.

Don suppressed a chuckle. "C'mere and let me help you fix that. You and I are on our own tomorrow afternoon. What d'you think of that?"

"Oh, boy!" shouted Roderick. "What're we going to do?"

"Boy things, I expect," said Don. "We'll think of something."

"Did you pick up your toys in the living room?" asked Gertrude.

"I think so," he replied. "Most of them anyway. Can I have some crusts?"

"May I have some, please," said Gertrude.

"May I have some, please," said Roderick.

"You may have a few, but we have to save some for the birds. Then you have to go to bed so you can be all rested up to play with Daddy tomorrow."

"Maybe I should go too," chuckled Don. "I'll need my strength to keep up with him."

"It'll be good exercise." Gertrude laughed. "Finish your snack, Roddy, and Daddy'll take you up to bed."

"By the way," said Don, "Jim called today. He wants us to go there for supper tomorrow evening."

"Oh, he's back, is he? That's good. That'll give me a nice break after the tea."

"Are you ready, Roddy? Want a piggy back ride?" Don bent down to accommodate his small son.

"Now don't get him too excited, or he won't go to sleep," said Gertrude.

"Duck your head," said Don to Roddy as he stooped to go through the kitchen door. They clattered up the stairs and into Roderick's bedroom where Don dumped the giggling Roddy onto his bed. "Want a story?"

"No, thank you," said Roderick. "The pretty lady's here. I think I'll just talk to her for awhile. She's very lonely."

"Maybe she's looking for Paulie," said Don.

"Paulie's not real, you know that!"

"And the pretty lady is?"

"Of course! She's sitting right there." Roderick pointed to the foot of the bed.

Don looked and saw nothing. "Well, don't talk too late," he said. He suppressed a shiver. "And don't let your imagination run away with you. I don't want to be summoned in the middle of the night to calm your nightmares."

"I won't. Good night, Daddy."

"Good night, Roderick. Sleep tight. Don't forget to say your prayers." Don returned to the kitchen, a puzzled frown on his face.

"What's the matter?" asked Gertrude as she wiped up the table.

"Roderick has such a wild imagination sometimes, that's all. He's up there now, talking to the pretty lady."

"Oh," said Gertrude. "He always talks to her."

"But isn't she the one he said he saw over at Amanda's that time?"

"Yes, d'you want some tea?" she asked.

"Tea would be very nice, and don't try to change the

subject," said Don.

She filled the kettle and plugged it in. "What was he saying?"

"Just that she's real and Paulie's not, and that she's lonely."

"It's likely all in his imagination," she said. "It can be pretty wild by times."

"Hm." Don let the subject drop.

The next afternoon Don let Gertrude and her packages out at the church. "I'll pick you up at five-thirty?"

"About that," said Gertrude. "If we get finished any earlier I can always get a ride, or call you. See you later." She slammed the car door and hurried into the church.

"So what do you want to do?" Don turned to Roderick who was strapped into his car seat in the back seat.

"Let's go to the playground."

"We'll have to go to the one in Victoria Park," said Don. "That's the only one that has swings that fit me." He pulled into traffic and headed toward the park. Roderick didn't reply.

In a few minutes Don parked the car and assisted Roderick out of his car seat. "It's nice and cool today so there's no one around. We'll have the swings to ourselves."

"Where does the sun go when it's not shining?" asked Roderick.

"On a day like today it hides behind the clouds, and at night when it's real dark, it's on the other side of the earth."

"Oh." Roderick digested this for a few moments. "Does it ever go out?"

Don helped him into the swing seat and began pushing him. "It never goes out. Pump your legs like you did the last time to keep yourself going. I'm going to swing too." He settled himself on the swing next to Roderick's and began to swing. "Let's see who can go higher."

Roderick pumped as hard as his little boy legs could pump. Don pretended to pump hard too. Roderick slowly gained on Don and finally passed him.

"I won! I won!" shouted Roderick. "I beat you, Daddy!" He dragged his feet and slowed himself down. "Let's go play pirates on the guns."

Don helped him out of the swing seat and he ran off toward the cannons at top speed. Don hurried after him. Suddenly Roderick came to a stop.

"I don't want to play pirates, Daddy. Let's swing some

more." He turned around and began to walk slowly back toward the swings.

"Why don't you want to play pirates all of a sudden?" Don took his hand.

Roderick shrugged one small shoulder. "Just don't."

"C'mon, now, Roddy, there must be a reason, and knowing you it'll probably be a pretty good one. Tell Daddy why you don't want to play pirates."

"The man with the funny hat's there," said Roderick. "I don't like him."

Don turned to look. There was no one there. "He's gone now. Anyway, I'm with you, and I won't let him hurt you."

"You couldn't stop him." Roderick looked Don squarely in the eyes.

"Well, he's gone now, so it's a moot point." Don repressed a shiver of concern for his son.

"What's a moot, Daddy?"

"It just means that the discussion is based on something that's not real any longer. Let's go check out those cannons and see if he's really gone." Don turned Roderick around and together they headed back toward the big guns. Roderick walked very slowly looking at his feet all the way.

"What's the matter, son?" asked Don.

"I'm afraid that if I look up I'll see him." Roderick continued to look at his feet.

"But there's no one there." Don searched with his eyes around the row of cannons.

Roderick looked up. "But he's right there, Daddy." Roderick clutched Don's leg. "Can't you see him?"

"I can't see him," said Don. "Show me where."

Roderick pointed. "Right there, by the second one." He grabbed Don's leg again.

"But there's no one there!"

"Yes, there is! Yes, there is!" persisted Roderick, "and he's looking at me!" He buried his face in Don's thigh.

"We'll go away from here then, and you can tell me all about it in a little while." He picked Roderick up and carried him back toward the car. "Let's go to the DQ and get some ice cream. How about that?"

"Okay." Roderick, crying, buried his face in his father's neck and hung onto him for dear life.

❖

Don bought them each a hot fudge sundae and they sat at a table by the window watching the cars go by as they ate. When Don judged that Roderick was sufficiently restored to his normal state, he asked, "Can you tell me about this man in the park now?"

Roderick looked up, his spoon poised for the last bite of ice cream that hadn't yet melted. "He's a man in a funny hat, and he's mean to little boys."

"What do you mean by a funny hat?"

"It looks kind of square, like a pirate's hat. You know, like Captain Hook's hat in my picture book."

"Oh, you mean three-cornered," said Don. "But those are very old hats, no one wears those any more."

"He does," said Roderick.

"Is he always by himself?"

"I never see anyone with him." Roderick picked up his bowl and drank the melted ice cream from it.

"Are there ever other people in the park when he's there?"

"Today there was just you and me, but the other day there was Mommy and me, and some ladies in long dresses, but they weren't with him. Mommy couldn't see him either."

"Did you tell Mommy about him?"

"Of course, I tell her everything. Can we go now?"

"If you want to. Where do you want to go next?"

"Let's go to the tea and see Mommy."

Don scooped up the last of his melted ice cream and sighed at the prospect of braving a church hall full of ladies in their best bib and tucker. "Whatever you want, son."

"Maybe she'll be ready to come home now."

Oh dear, thought Don. He peered around the edge of the doorway looking for Gertrude. He could feel his face getting warm.

"Why, Dr. Harvey, how nice to see you!" squealed Amy Lovet. "I hope you've come to enjoy the tea." She grabbed Don's arm and began dragging him toward an empty tea table. "Is this your boy? My, he's certainly grown. Here, I'll just seat you at one of Gertrude's tables."

"Thank you," said Don. The uncomfortable glow in his face began to subside. I can deal with anything as long as it's professional in nature, but these ladies' days I just can't handle, he thought. I hope Gertrude isn't long coming.

"Now you just wait right there, and I'll tell Gertrude

you're here," Amy cackled. "I'll only be a minute." She trotted off toward the kitchen, her portly body supported on tiny feet in too small shoes.

Presently Gertrude emerged from the kitchen looking hot and ruffled. "I'm surprised to see you here," she said.

"Roderick wanted to come and see if you were ready to come home." Don's colour had nearly returned to normal. "Does that Amy one ever talk in normal tones?" he whispered.

Gertrude laughed. "I've never heard her do anything but cackle and gush. D'you guys want some sandwiches?"

"I don't, thanks," said Don, "and I don't think he can eat anything either. We just got through at DQ. Are you going to be ready to come home soon?"

Gertrude surveyed the hall. "I think so. The tea time is nearly over, and this place seems to be clearing out. I still have to help clean up the kitchen, but that shouldn't take too long."

Roderick finished his observation of the hall. "Mommy, we saw that man in the funny hat today. He looked at me cross."

"Yes," said Don, "we need to talk about that when we

go home. I think you may have something to tell me, eh?"

Gertrude swallowed the curious lump that had suddenly formed in her throat. "I'll be ready in about fifteen minutes." She hurried off to the kitchen again.

"I want you to lay down and have a nap, Roderick. We're all going out to Uncle Jim's for supper this evening, and I want you to be in good humour."

"I know, you really just want to talk to Daddy, and you don't want me around."

"Smart kid! Now up the stairs," said Gertrude. "Pull the blanket over you, too," she called after him.

"Want some tea?" She returned to the kitchen and closed the door behind herself.

"Thanks," said Don. If Roderick has the gift too…, he thought.

"The tea was a great success, we made over seven hundred dollars." She filled the kettle and plugged it in.

"I'm sorry, what did you say?" he asked.

"I said, we made over seven hundred dollars," repeated Gertrude. "You don't look very happy. What's on your mind?" As if I didn't know already, she thought.

"Why didn't you tell me about Roderick? He's my son too, you know," said Don. His misery was evident in his face.

Gertrude sighed. "I'm sorry, I only just found out myself, and I didn't know how to tell you. It's hard enough for you to have one psychic in the house, never mind two."

"You might at least have hinted."

"I thought sure you had already caught on when he was babbling about the pretty lady. I thought you were just taking time to digest it before we did talk about it." She rose to put down the tea to steep.

"I thought the pretty lady was just another Paulie, a figment of his imagination, especially since you didn't appear to have seen her."

"It's true, I didn't see her, but I told you then, I wasn't looking for anything." She poured tea into mugs and set one in front of him. She sat down at the corner of the table and propped her feet in Don's lap. "Rub them for me, please, they're worn out."

Don began to massage her feet. "What about the man in the park?"

Gertrude peered at him over the rim of her mug. "I didn't see him either."

"Roddy says that the man is mean to little boys, and that he looked right at him today. He was really frightened of him."

"I know he is, but there's not much I can do about that, except avoid the place."

Don blew on his tea to cool it. He sat in silence for several minutes. "Maybe that's what you need to do, at least for the time being," he said at last, then lapsed into silence again. After a few minutes of deep thought he asked, "Can this guy harm Roderick?"

"I don't think so," she said. "He'd have to be more than just a ghost if he were to do any real damage on this plane."

"What about the pretty lady? Can she do him any harm?"

"From what Roderick tells me, she's just a ghost looking for some company, and she's attracted to children. At any rate he's not afraid of her. I think he rather likes her." Gertrude reached for the tea pot. "Another spot?" she asked as she refilled her own cup.

"Half a cup." Don held out his mug. "Why can't you see

these people? I thought if you were a sensitive you could see everything."

Gertrude sipped her tea. "Not necessarily. In the pretty lady's case I wasn't looking, though I did catch a glimpse of her the other evening up in Roderick's room, but my presence seemed to dissipate her energy. I don't know why."

"What about the man?"

Gertrude frowned and shook her head. "I don't know about him. If he's what I think he is, a true spirit like Larry, he may be able to prevent me from seeing him. He'll know that I'm a sensitive just by looking at me. If he's a bad man, like Roddy seems to think he is, he may be up to no good and not want me interfering, as he knows I will."

"What's the difference between him and the 'pretty lady?'"

"She's just a remnant of psychic energy left over from a particularly unhappy life, and if he's a spirit, he has a life of his own in the spirit realm and can influence his surroundings just the same as we can here. Of course, he may be just a very strong ghost too, I don't know."

"Can you find out?"

Gertrude shrugged. "I can try. Maybe Mary Ann'll help me this evening, but don't hope for too much. If he's a spirit he may not want me to know who he is."

Don felt a shiver go over his skin. "How're we going to protect our son?" he asked.

"We'll stay away from the park for the time being. In a few months this may all blow over. I can guard him psychically to some extent. You have to remember, too, that Roddy doesn't like that man, and he's not going to seek him out. If anything he'll come running to us if he's frightened by him."

"Frightened by who?" asked Roderick from the kitchen doorway.

"By whom, honey. The man in the park." Gertrude scooped the sleep-rosy child into her arms for a hug. "That wasn't a very long nap."

"I slept fast," said Roderick. "Can we go out to Uncle Jim's now? I don't want to think about the man in the park. I want to see Betsy."

CHAPTER 8

Betsy greeted them with a woof as they climbed out of the car in Jim's yard.

"Well, Betsy, did you have a good trip?" Gertrude ruffled Betsy's ears.

Betsy's large plumy tail wagged even faster, and she was hard put to keep her great paws on the ground.

"You're looking more and more like your master every day." Don patted the other end of Betsy.

"Hi, guys." Jim's massive body filled the door frame. "C'mon in, supper's almost ready. Mary Ann's bringing dessert. She just called, she'll be here in a few minutes. G'day, Roderick, how are you?" he bent down and shook hands with Roderick.

"I'm fine, thank you. D'you know what we did today, Uncle Jim?"

"I have no idea," said Jim. "Tell me."

"Mommy had a tea, and Daddy and I went to the park, and then we had some ice cream, and then we went to the tea too." Roderick stopped for breath. "Oh, yes, and we saw the man with the funny hat by the cannons."

"Great Scott! Half of that would have been enough," said Jim. "Will you still have room for supper?"

Roderick patted his stomach. "I think so."

Just then Mary Ann's car pulled into the yard with a spray of gravel and pink dust.

"Go on in and make yourself at home, and I'll go and see if Mary Ann needs any help."

"Sorry I'm late," called Mary Ann from across the yard. She hopped out of her ancient vehicle. "The cat caught a bird and dragged it into the house and it wasn't quite dead and it got away. It was bleeding badly and I had to wait until it got too weak and fell off the curtain rod and died. Then I had to clean up the blood spots and bury the poor creature. Thank goodness I already had my cake made and covered up, there were feathers everywhere." She ran out of breath as she followed the others into the kitchen. "Jim's bringing the cake in. You're looking glum tonight, Don. What's wrong?"

Don frowned and Gertrude replied, "He just found out about our little friend's g-i-f-t, and he has to get used to the idea yet."

"Oh." Mary Ann was momentarily silenced.

"You sound as if you already knew about it," said Don.

"Molly let it slip when he was born."

"I suppose you told Gertrude all about it?"

"I did not," said Mary Ann. "Molly wasn't supposed to tell me and she swore me to secrecy, so I couldn't tell anyone."

"And she didn't," said Gertrude. "If she had I would have told you long ago."

"Sit in children, and don't fight," boomed Jim from the pantry. "We'll talk about this after supper."

"Talk about what, Mommy?" asked Roderick as Gertrude piled cushions on his chair and plopped him on top of the pile. "Am I going to get a present?"

"No," said Gertrude, "you're going to get your supper."

She pushed his chair in to the table and sat down beside him.

"But you just spelled gift," he protested. "Doesn't gift mean present?"

Gertrude rolled her eyes. "Sometimes it does, but not in this case. Do you want to say grace?"

"Okay," he said, distracted for the moment.

Grace was said, and Roderick's plate was filled. "I didn't know he could spell," mouthed Gertrude to the others as she passed the mashed potatoes to Mary Ann. "It won't be safe to say anything any more."

Supper was eaten with a minimum of conversation. Mary Ann's cake was a delight to the eye and to the palate. Jim handed large mugs of coffee around to everyone except Roderick who got a mug of milk with a tablespoon of coffee in it just to pretend.

"So what's this about the man with the funny hat?" Jim took his place again and leaned forward on his elbows.

"His nibs appears to be able to see the same things that Gertrude and Mary Ann can see," said Don. "He says there's a man in the park who doesn't like little boys, and he's afraid of him. As far as I can tell from his description of the hat, it's a tricorn. He said it was like Captain Hook's in his picture book."

"I wonder who he is?" said Mary Ann.

"I have no idea," said Gertrude. "I have yet to see him."

"That's strange," said Mary Ann. "Have you talked to Molly about him?"

Gertrude sighed. "I haven't had time, or energy either, to even say hello to Molly."

"I was talking to her yesterday and she wasn't in very good humour. Guilty conscience, I guess, from having told me about him." Mary Ann nodded in Roderick's direction, where he lay sprawled on the floor playing with his dump truck, carrying bits of bark from the wood box from place to place.

"Want to try to contact her tonight?"

"Sure," said Mary Ann, "if it won't bother Roddy."

"He likely won't even know what's going on."

"Want to bet?" said Jim and Don in chorus.

"No." Gertrude laughed. "I guess I don't." She relaxed in her chair and focused inward. "Are you coming with me, Mary Ann?" She sighed, and lapsed into trance.

"Molly! Molly! Can you hear me?" she called mentally.

Mary Ann was soon with her and together they called again. At last Molly appeared in her customary place on the clock shelf.

"It's about time!" said Gertrude. "I'd hate to see how long you'd be if it were an emergency."

"It's about time," mimicked Molly. "You took me away from a very interesting gathering. I was talking to Josephine. She was telling me about Napoleon being away from home so much, and how hard it was for her."

"Where's Lucy this evening?" asked Mary Ann.

"Gone somewhere with Larry, I expect. She has her hands full with keeping that fellow in line, I'll tell you. So what did you want?"

"Who's the man in the park?" asked Gertrude.

Molly frowned. "What man? What park? Be more specific!"

"Roderick keeps seeing a man in a three-cornered hat in Victoria Park, down by the cannons. He's afraid of him. He says he's mean to little boys."

"Hm," said Molly. "I don't know. The description's still pretty vague. Probably just some rogue ghost who likes to glare at little boys and frighten them."

"I don't think so," said Gertrude. "After all it's Roddy we're talking about, and you know him, he's not afraid of too much."

"Oh, yes, Mr. Precocious," said Molly. "Well, Larry might know. You can always call him."

"What d'you think, Mary Ann? Should we call Larry tonight?"

Mary Ann shrugged. "It doesn't make much difference if we call him tonight or tomorrow, we'll be disturbing him at something."

"You're right." Gertrude gathered her energy to call to Larry through the ether. "Larry! Larry!"

A faint breeze announced Larry's arrival on the clock shelf, followed a moment later by a breathless, dithering Lucy. "Oh, Larry, you know you shouldn't have said that to the elder. Especially not to that one. He has no sense of humour."

"He's a nincompoop," boomed Larry, "and he never did have a sense of humour. What do you want?" He turned his attention to Gertrude.

"Good evening," said Gertrude. "I need some information."

"Don't you always," barked Larry.

"Not always," said Gertrude. "Sometimes I just like to chat."

"Well, you've never invited me to a party, have you?"

"No, but then I don't go to very many parties, and besides you'd probably be bored."

"Let me be the judge of that," he roared. "Now, what was it you want?"

"I want to know who the man in Victoria Park is."

"What man? Be more specific!"

"The one that Roderick can see and I can't."

"Must be a spirit if you can't see him," said Larry.

"Roddy's afraid of him. He says he's mean to little boys."

"I'll check it out," said Larry. "Back in a flash."

"If that man really is a spirit, will Larry be able to see him if he doesn't want him to?" asked Gertrude.

"I expect so," said Molly. Then in mysterious tones, and with a twitch of her left eyebrow, she said, "Larry has ways."

Larry returned almost immediately. "That's Slippery Jack Black. Roderick'll do well to be afraid of him. He practically eats little boys for breakfast."

"What's that supposed to mean?" said Molly.

116

"That means," said Larry, "that Slippery Jack kidnaps children and sells them to whoever has the right amount of money. It doesn't matter what they want them for either."

"What's he doing in Charlottetown?" Gertrude's voice rose in alarm. Those in the physical looked at one another with questioning expressions. "Can he hurt Roddy?"

"He's hiding out. It got too hot for him down the New England coast, and he needed a place to hole up in for awhile. He can't do a whole lot to Roderick besides frighten him, but in case he can, you'd be well advised to stay away from the park for a few months. They hanged him, you know."

Gertrude suppressed a shudder. "How long's he going to be here? Is he in the history books?"

"No, he never left any trace of himself. He couldn't write, and he was always on the move, and when they caught up with him they hanged him on the spot without benefit of the law. No one knew who did it, and no one cared. He was a very bad man. For his sins, the celestial court required him to relive that life over and over again until he understands the evil he's done." Larry shook his head. "He's a slow learner."

"Well, I'm going to search in the library anyway," said Gertrude. "There might be something on him. By his hat, he must have been here in the very early days of the city."

"Don't let the hat fool you," said Larry. "He acquired that from a colonial corpse, long after the corpse was no longer. He liked hats."

"Yuck!" said the girls in chorus. "That disgusting man."

"You said it." Larry stretched his tall frame, and preened the large red plume in his hat. "Well, I'm off." He faded from view with Lucy following.

"So'm I," said Molly.

"Thanks, Molly," called Gertrude and Mary Ann after Molly's rapidly fading form.

"Mommy, who were those people you were talking to?" Roderick leaned against Gertrude's legs as she came out of trance.

Gertrude stretched and yawned. "Friends of mine," she said. "You'll probably be meeting them someday."

"Why were they so cross at you, and why were they sitting on the clock shelf?"

"They weren't cross at me, that's just the way they talk, and they were sitting on the clock shelf because that's where they like to sit when they come to visit."

"Can I sit on the clock shelf too?"

"Under no circumstances are you ever to sit up there!" said Gertrude.

CHAPTER 9

Kitty jumped up on the little table on the landing and knocked over Amanda's prized Shepherd's Purse. It fell with a crash, scattering dirt and leaves, and small yellow purse-like flowers. Kitty jumped down again and sniffed at the remains of the plant, then padded softly away to the bathroom. She jumped up on the vanity and perched on the edge of the basin, ears and whiskers forward, waiting for the next drop to fall. The taps were tight and no drop fell. Kitty leaned into the basin, her rump and tail held high as she licked the residue of water from around the drain. A bird flew against the window and settled on the sill outside. Kitty jumped to the toilet seat and braced herself on the inside window sill chattering her teeth, and emitting small cries of kitty anguish when she discovered that the bird was out of reach.

Downstairs Amanda and Alec were just finishing supper. "What is that beast into now?" said Amanda when she heard the flower pot fall. Presently they heard her chattering and crying. "There must be a bird on the window sill up there," she remarked. "Sometimes I'm sorry I let her stay."

"I thought you didn't have any choice about it?" said Alec. "By the way, I found the hole where she was getting in from outside. She must have been doing it for some time, I could see where she'd made a bed on that pile of burlap sacks I threw down there when we moved here."

Amanda began scraping the plates. "Did you find where she gets up here from?"

"Not yet, but that really doesn't matter if she can't get in from outside in the first place."

"Well, I'm relieved. I was afraid of her getting in here unsupervised after the baby was born and maybe harming it."

"You don't believe that old wives' tale about cats sucking

a baby's breath, do you?"

Amanda began filling the dish pan. "No, of course not. But I know they like to sleep close to a baby's face because of the warmth, and they can easily smother a newborn. Remember that woman over in Kinkora. She got there just in time to shoo the cat away. She sat up day and night after that until the baby was big enough to turn over by itself. I heard she was a nervous wreck by that time, and the baby was a spoiled brat from having its mother there night and day."

"Well, we won't let that happen, will we, love." Alec smiled and picked up the tea towel and gave her a peck on the cheek in passing.

"I hope not." Amanda plunged the silverware into the hot soapy water. She began washing forks and was lost in thought for some minutes.

"What're you thinking about?" asked Alec.

"I was just imagining having a baby here all the time. It'll seem strange after all this time without one."

"We'll get used to it, I expect."

"I guess we'll have to, won't we!"

"We'll soon have to think about getting the nursery

ready. It's only six months away now. I wonder if Gertrude and Don have any nursery furniture left yet?"

"Have you thought what we might call it?"

"I don't know, I haven't thought that far ahead. I'm still getting used to the idea of becoming a father." Alec rinsed the cutlery and began drying it piece by piece.

"Well, I've thought about it a lot. I think if we have a boy we should name him Ian Alexander."

Alec laughed. "And if it's a girl?"

"Janet Elizabeth."

"Well," said Alec, "that certainly should satisfy the family. Your mother and my father and both of us."

"Just our middle names, and those're names it can live with," Amanda pointed out. "Besides, I rather like the combinations. What would you call it?"

"Those names are fine with me. I was actually dreading the business of picking out a name for it. You know the fuss my mother made when young Jacob was born and they didn't name him after anyone."

Amanda laughed. "And she still goes on about it, and him thirteen. You'd think she'd have let it go by now." She wiped off the counter. "It's so nice to have you to myself for an evening." She hung up the dish cloth and turned to snuggle into Alec's arms. "I was beginning to resent the Social Services Department, you know."

Alec rested his chin on top of her smooth head. "Well, I'm finally getting caught up. I should be seeing the last of that backlog of work by the end of June." His glance strayed out the window to the far end of the garden. "It seems we have a mist rolling in tonight." The mist gathered itself on the dusk-wrapped lawn and moved along the fence to the corner of the yard where it passed through the pickets and dissipated. Alec grew stiff with apprehension and astonishment.

Amanda raised her head in alarm. "What's the matter, Alec?"

Alec stood silently staring out the kitchen window, his mouth hanging slackly open. He swallowed hard, then said, "I don't believe what I just saw!" He continued to stare out the window.

Amanda turned to look too. "I don't see anything."

"It's gone now."

"What was it?"

"I think I just saw a ghost!"

"Where? What was it like? Did it look like a real person?"

Alec swallowed hard again. "Och, it was just mist forming like it does some evenings."

"But did it look like anything?"

Alec finally turned to look at her. "No, it was just a mist, although, with a little imagination, I could have made it into a woman in long skirts."

Amanda laughed nervously. "Well, at least it didn't come into the house."

"Let's go sit in the living room," said Alec. "I'll pull the curtains in here so we won't have to look out there any more this evening."

"I think I'd like to leave the lights on, too," said Amanda. She waited for Alec to close the curtains. Together they walked across the hallway to the living room, turning lights on as they went.

"I hate to think what the light bill will be this month if we keep the lights on all the time," said Amanda.

"Just for tonight." Alec settled himself on the chesterfield and propped his feet on the coffee table. "C'mere you." He held out his arms to her and she snuggled into them. "Did you ever hear your Aunt Martha talk about ghosts?"

"D'you mean here in the house?"

Alec shrugged. "Mm, not just in the house. Anywhere on the property."

"Not that I recall. Of course you remember how feisty Aunt Martha was. If there'd been even a suggestion of a ghost here she'd have put the run to it first, and asked questions afterwards, and pity help the prankster who tried one out on her. Besides, she didn't believe in ghosts."

"Hm." Alec was silent for a few minutes pondering over the rational explanations for the strange mist in the garden. "You don't suppose it was a prank, do you?"

"Who'd do a thing like that to us? We're friendly with all our neighbours, and most of them have known me for years."

"Maybe it isn't a neighbour. Didn't you tell me one time that that wheeler-dealer, Nicks, wanted to buy this house?"

"He was after Aunt Martha to sell for a long time, but she wouldn't. I think he wanted to turn it into apartments."

"D'you know him?"

"I met him once or twice when I was a teenager and staying the summer with Aunt Martha. He was kind of a shifty character."

"D'you think he'd be at that kind of work?"

"You mean manufacturing ghosts?"

"For instance."

Amanda thought for a moment. "I honestly don't think he has that kind of imagination. For all his fancy dealings in the housing industry, he's really kind of a stupid man."

"Could he have put someone else up to it?"

"Maybe, but I don't think so. As I said, he's just not that subtle. I don't think he'd think of such a thing."

"Well, I'm going to check the garden for signs of trespass in the morning, just in case it was something human after all." He pulled Amanda closer to him and patted her gently on the abdomen. "How's little Ian-Janet getting on?"

"Janet-Ian's doing just fine as far as I can tell. Mommy's doing well too. She doesn't even suffer from morning sickness."

Amanda opened her eyes to the darkness of the very early morning. A faint glow from the street lamps on the other street illuminated the windows. The breeze from the harbour whispered and sighed in the maple tree outside. She lay there thinking about their talk of the evening before. Beside her Alec slept quietly. She watched the even rise and fall of his chest in silhouette with the faint light from the window. Her thoughts turned happily to the baby in her womb. Her heart felt full to bursting with the joy of it.

Gradually she became aware of faint sounds from the rest of the house. It's just the cat, she decided, nothing to worry about. She began to drift off to sleep. The sounds persisted, and became more distinct. Alec said he put the cat out, she thought. I wonder if the wretch found another way in? I'd better go and see what she's up to. She rolled to a sitting position, swung her legs over the side of the bed, and stuck her feet into her pink slippers. Alec turned and muttered in his sleep. "I'll be back in a minute, love," she whispered. She pulled on her quilted robe and made her way carefully to the door.

In the hallway the sounds resolved themselves into the squeak of a rocker on a wooden floor. Amanda's attention was drawn to the door of the maid's room. It stood ajar, a glow from the street lights on the side street outlined it. That's too bright for street lights, she thought. She moved closer to the door and reached out a tentative hand toward the knob. Faint sobs reached her ears and the rocking continued. She felt herself compelled to open the door wide and look into the room.

The scene before her eyes had an unearthly quality to it. A woman of about her own age sat in a rocking chair weeping and rocking. She held a baby's smock, her restless hands worried at the lace on it. Occasionally she wiped her streaming eyes with the hem of it. Amanda stared in fascinated horror. The woman looked up, her hands continued folding and refolding the lace on the smock. She stared directly at Amanda, then rose and held out her hand beseechingly as she moved toward her. Amanda was momentarily paralysed with terror. "Ah, ah, ah!" She couldn't even scream. The woman continued toward her. Amanda turned to run, catching her slipper on the hem of her long robe as she fled across the landing. She found her voice in a ghastly scream as she lost her footing. Her fall down the stairs was mercifully shrouded in her loss of consciousness.

Alec's feet hit the floor at the first sound of her scream. He arrived on the landing in time to see Amanda roll to a stop in the hallway below. She didn't move. He went down over the stairs in three giant leaps. "Amanda! Amanda!" She gave no response. I mustn't try to move her, part of his brain was telling him. Help, I must get help! Amanda moaned. At least she's still alive! He hurried to the telephone and tried to look up the number of Neil's Ambulance Service with shaking hands. He dropped the book and tried again. His brain seemed to be on hold. Amanda moaned again. He gave up his search and called the operator.

Amanda's awareness returned slowly. She opened her eyes briefly to the glare from the examination lights above her stretcher. She clamped them shut again. Why do I ache so? Her mind kept a close guard on her thoughts. Why can't I think right? What's happened to me? An unfamiliar stickiness between her legs caught her attention. My baby! What's happened to my baby? "Alec!" she shrieked.

The nurse jumped. "Alec's right outside. You're okay now. Just let me check your vital signs, and then he can come in." But Alec was already in.

"My baby, my baby," moaned Amanda.

"Hush, honey," soothed Alec. "The baby's still there, and you're all right too." He stroked her forehead.

Amanda began to cry. "Oh, Alec, I hurt so, and I'm bleeding. I just know I am."

"You've had a slight hemorrhage, but it seems to have stopped now," said the nurse. "Now don't upset yourself and everything should be all right. You've had a nasty fall."

"Fall?" said Amanda.

"Yes," said Alec, "you fell down the stairs."

"I did? That must be why I hurt so."

"You've sprained your ankle and cracked your wrist. The doctor wants you on bed rest for the next two weeks. What were you doing out on the landing anyway?"

Amanda's brain refused to function past a certain point. "I heard the cat and I went to see what she was up to. After that I don't remember anything."

"But the cat wasn't even in the house. I put her out myself before we went up to bed."

"I know, but I thought it was her, all the same."

"Now, Amanda, that doesn't make sense," said Alec.

"I know," she sighed. "Nothing makes sense anymore." She drifted off into a light sleep.

The noisy clatter of the food trolley awakened her the next morning. Where am I? she wondered briefly before awareness returned. Anxiety gripped her. She ran her hand over the slight bulge in her abdomen. She breathed a sigh of relief. At least I haven't lost you, she thought.

"So you're awake at last," said the nurse as she came into the room carrying Amanda's breakfast tray. "D'you feel like eating anything?" She set the tray on the over-bed table and rolled up the head of the bed.

"Am I allowed to sit up?" asked Amanda.

"Yes, but you're not allowed out of bed for a few days, until we see how baby's doing."

"Where's Alec?"

"He went home about four o'clock. You were asleep and were doing okay, so he went home to get a little rest. He said he'd be back first thing."

"Poor Alec, he's such a sweetheart, I hate to have worried him like this." Amanda sighed.

"Well, it couldn't be helped, I guess. Eat your breakfast now, you're going to need your strength for the next few days."

Amanda investigated the contents of her tray, and began to pick at her food. Why was I out on the landing in the middle of the night? she wondered. I know I told Alec that I was seeing what the cat was up to, but I don't think that's the real reason. She nibbled on a piece of crisp bacon. I remember getting up and going out into the hall, but after that it's kind of blurry. A frown crossed her features and stayed there for some minutes.

Alec found it still there when he arrived a few minutes later. "You're looking worried." He settled himself on the straight chair by the bed. "Are you feeling any better?"

"I think the bleeding's stopped, but I'm awfully sore. I hurt in places I didn't know I owned."

"Well, that'll pass soon enough. At least you're all right, and the baby too." He patted her hand. "Now, have you remembered anything more about last night?"

Amanda shrugged. "Not really. I just remember thinking about the cat. I woke up, and I was just lying there thinking about us, and the baby, and feeling very happy about everything, and then I thought I heard the cat up to something so I went to investigate."

"But the cat was outside, I put her out myself before I went up to bed," said Alec.

"I know, I thought of that, but I thought she'd found another way into the basement, and we never have found how she gets up from there."

"And did you find her?"

Amanda frowned. "No, I don't remember finding her. The last thing I remember doing was going to the door of the maid's room."

"Why'd you go there?"

Amanda concentrated hard for a moment. "That's where I thought the cat was. The door was ajar and I could hear creaking noises coming from there."

"Did you investigate?"

"I think so. I remember going to the door and giving it a push. It started to open. I think it opened all the way." Amanda's eyes grew round with remembered horror. Her bacon fell from nerveless fingers. "Oh, my God! She's coming toward me!" she gasped. "I've got to get away!" She made to leap out of bed.

Alec took her by the shoulders and gently shook her back to present awareness. "Amanda! Amanda! It's okay, honey. I'm here now and it's all over, and nothing's going to hurt you anymore." He helped her settle back on the pillows. Her eyes still held the blank look of terror, her breathing was ragged and her body was tense. She began to cry. Alec gathered her into his arms and rocked her gently back and forth.

"Whatever did you see?" he asked, when her wild sobbing had eased.

She buried her face in the curve of his shoulder. "Oh, Alec, it was h-horrible! She came at me with her hand out. She wanted something from me."

"She?"

"A woman in long skirts. She was sitting in the rocking chair, rocking and weeping, and folding and unfolding a little dress. She was so sad." Amanda felt the tears well up in her eyes again.

"But there's no furniture in that room yet."

"I know, but she was sitting in a rocking chair." Amanda shrugged feebly. "I don't know how." She began to cry again.

"You said she wanted something?"

"Yes, but I don't know what. She was so unhappy. She looked up, and saw me, and got up and came toward me with her hand out, and that's when I turned and ran away. After that I don't remember anything." She scrubbed at her tears with the heel of her hand. Alec continued to rock her.

"Did she seem real to you?"

"She was real, all right," said Amanda. "She certainly wasn't a figment of my imagination." She sniffed hugely and reached for a tissue.

Alec frowned. "Was there anything strange about her appearance at all?"

Amanda thought for a moment. "You know, now that you mention it, there was a kind of glow in the room. I thought it was just the street lights outside, but come to think about it, those street lights aren't right by that window, so it couldn't have been that."

"Could she have been a ghost?"

"No, of course not," said Amanda, "there's no such things as ghosts."

"You're probably right." Alec laughed. "It was probably just shadows and maybe you were sleep-walking. I hear strange things happen to women when they're pregnant."

"Oh, you!" said Amanda. "The next thing you'll be telling me that I'm 'delicate.'"

I'd better not tell her what I found in that room this morning, thought Alec as he crossed the parking lot a little later that morning. I don't want to frighten her again. The old-fashioned lace baby dress lay hidden in the basement on a shelf behind the furnace, where Alec had put it when he came home that morning and found it lying on the floor of the maid's room.

CHAPTER 10

A lec mulled over the problem all day, to the detriment of his work. It is a problem, he thought to himself. It's not just an annoyance anymore. She really did see something in that room, and I have the dress to prove it. What am I going to do? We can't very well move out until all this is solved, and I can't take her home to a haunted house. Why can't I see what she sees? What does that woman want from Amanda? How are we going to get rid of her? His thoughts continued on the merry-go-round of his mind. At three o'clock he finally gave up and went home.

The brief walk from the office to his house cleared his head somewhat, and he felt better for the breath of fresh air. I'm going to make myself a cup of tea, and sit down and make a list of what I know for fact about this, he thought. Maybe I can see a solution that way. He went into the kitchen and began filling the kettle. The telephone shrilled in the hallway. It was Gertrude wanting to talk to Amanda.

"I'm sorry, Gertrude, but she's in the hospital right now. She's had a fall, and they're keeping her for observation."

"Is the baby okay?" asked Gertrude.

"As far as we know, the baby's fine. They just want to make sure, so she's going to be there for awhile."

"Well!" said Gertrude, thinking of her dream of the previous night. "Is she on maternity?"

"She's in that private room by the nurses' station. They wanted to keep her away from other mothers and their babies in case she lost ours. She's allowed visitors and I know she'd be awfully glad for the company if you want to go and see her."

"I'll do that," said Gertrude. "Is there anything I can bring her?"

"I don't know of anything, but you might ask her when you see her."

The kettle whistled from the kitchen. "My kettle's on the boil, I have to go now," said Alec.

Gertrude laughed. "I can hear it from here. I'll keep in touch."

It was some minutes after Alec had sat down with his cup of tea, and his pencil and paper, to make his list, that he thought of Gertrude and her job with Jim. *I wonder if he's legitimate? I wonder if he can help?* He looked down at his list of two items. *I'm certainly not making any headway.*

He went to the telephone and dialled the Harvey number. Gertrude answered.

He greeted her then said: "I think I may have something to talk to you about regarding your work. May I come calling after visiting hours?"

"Certainly," said Gertrude. "Roderick'll be in bed by that time so we can talk freely. Shall I invite Jim too?"

"Oh, no," said Alec. "It may not mean a thing, and I feel that the fewer people who know about this the better."

Gertrude laughed. "I know what you mean. It feels as if it's just crazy, doesn't it?"

Alec let out the breath that he hadn't realized he'd been holding. "It sure does!"

"We'll see you this evening, then."

Now how does she know how it feels? wondered Alec,

as he hung up the phone. He shrugged mentally. She's probably learned from other people's experience. I must get that little dress and take it with me, in case I need to prove my point. He trudged down the stairs. The clay floor gave the cellar the smell of stored vegetables and damp earth. It evoked memories of his childhood helping his grandmother clean the roots off the potatoes in the spring so they'd last until the new crop was dug. It had been a peaceful job working side by side with her. A twist of his wrist and the tight slide of his thumb against the skin of the potato broke the roots off cleanly. He'd earned a whole dime for his efforts, but it was the sense of contentment that he treasured.

He made his way over to the furnace and squeezed himself into the space behind it. Reaching up to the shelf where he'd hidden the dress, his hand encountered nothing. Now where'd that thing go, he thought. I know I put it up here. He craned his neck to see if it was farther back on the shelf. Nothing, not even a mark in the dust to show that he'd been there only this morning. That dratted cat's taken it away for a bed. He didn't remember until much later that evening that there were no cat tracks on the shelf either.

❖

A visibly anxious Alec accepted a cup of tea from Gertrude that evening. They were seated at the kitchen table. "It's the best place for a serious discussion." Gertrude passed the plate of cookies to Alec. "Lots of light makes the situation seem less fantastical. So what seems to be the problem at your house?"

"I don't know if I can explain it adequately," began Alec. "Strange things have been happening there lately."

"Things like what?"

"Oh, strange mists in the garden, noises that we can't explain, the cat getting into the house from the basement without us being able to find out how. And now Amanda's fall. I tried to make a list of the occurrences to see if I could make some kind of sense out of it, but as you can see I wasn't very successful." He handed the crumpled list to Gertrude. "I only got as far as two points."

"These are two important points," said Gertrude. She showed the paper to Don. "Why'd you start with the mist in the garden?"

"I don't know. It just seemed reasonable to start at the

beginning. I can only relate what Amanda tells me about her experiences, but I can describe my own."

"So Amanda doesn't see the same things that you do?" said Don.

"It seems not, although she did see a mist in the garden, just not the same one that I did."

"So there are actually two separate incidents with mist?" asked Gertrude. "When'd Amanda see hers?"

"It was while I was away a few weeks ago. She saw it in the day time. She didn't tell me about it until the evening that I saw mine. She said it just kind of gathered itself into the left-hand corner of the yard down by the back fence and then dissipated. It was raining that day so she didn't think too much about it when it happened, until I saw the same thing yesterday evening."

"Could you tell from her description if the two events were identical?" asked Don.

Alec sipped his tea and considered the question. "No, I don't think they were exactly the same. She said hers just formed and dissipated, and mine took on shape and moved across the back of the yard before it went through the fence and disappeared."

"You say yours took on shape," said Gertrude. "What kind of shape?"

Alec laughed embarrassedly. "It's like I said to Amanda, with a little imagination I could see a lady in long skirts!"

"Hm," said Gertrude. "It could be a ghost, but on the other hand, it might really be just a configuration of mist. I wonder why the back of the garden? Is there anything down there?"

"Nothing but a bunch of weeds and overgrown bushes. The fence's falling down back there. I guess I'll have to get after it pretty soon. It needs to be cleaned out and replanted. I just haven't had time to do it yet."

"What does Amanda think of all this?" Don reached for another cookie. "Does she think it's ghosts?"

"I don't know what she thinks at this point," said Alec. "She's still denying the existence of ghosts, but I don't see how she can after what happened last night."

"What did happen last night?" asked Gertrude.

"She said she woke up and was lying there thinking about the baby and she started hearing noises in the house. She thought it was the cat up to something in the maid's room, and went to investigate. She said she saw a woman in a rocking chair crying and folding a baby dress. The woman got up and reached for her. She turned to run and stepped on the hem of her dressing gown and fell down the stairs. She didn't remember at first why she'd even gotten out of bed."

"Does she remember now?" asked Don.

"Unfortunately," said Alec. "It's a good thing I was there when she did remember, she was terrified all over again."

"That's often the way with head injuries," said Don. "At first they don't remember anything, then it all comes back in a rush."

"But she wasn't head injured," said Alec. "She sprained her ankle and cracked her wrist. She has a lot of bruises and sore muscles, but she didn't hit her head."

"Could what she saw be a result of her pregnancy and fluctuating hormone levels?" Gertrude poured more tea into everyone's cup without asking.

"I don't think so," said Alec. "When I got home from the hospital, I looked in the maid's room and found the little dress on the floor." He shrugged. "How do you explain that?"

"A prankster?" said Gertrude and Don at the same time.

"How would a prankster get into the house? The doors and windows were all locked."

"Amanda said the other day that old Nicks was trying to buy the house from Martha. D'you suppose he put someone up to something?"

Alec sighed. "We talked about that yesterday evening and Amanda says she doesn't think he has enough imagination for something like that."

"He might not, but his gofers might be wily enough to think of it," said Gertrude. "I lived in his apartment house on the other side of town before Don and I got married, and I got the impression that he was a pretty slippery character."

"Yeah, but Amanda seems to think he lacks the subtlety to dream up anything like that, never mind setting someone else to carrying it out."

Gertrude shrugged. "But that's just it. Maybe he didn't dream it up. Maybe he just gave free rein to someone to get you guys out one way or another."

"I suppose you're right," said Alec. He sighed, his tiredness evident in the deepened lines on his face. "That would explain the baby dress I found on the floor in there."

"What did you do with the dress?" asked Gertrude. "Can you show it to us?"

"That's another strange thing, I'm as sure as I'm sitting here, that I put it down on the shelf behind the furnace this morning. I didn't want Amanda to find it and become frightened all over again, so I hid it, and when I went back this evening to get it to bring it over here, it was gone."

"D'you suppose the cat might have taken it off someplace?" asked Gertrude.

"She might have. I thought of that. It may not be significant at all." He sat rethinking his earlier activities. He suddenly gave a slight gasp. "I just realized, it can't be the cat, there were no cat tracks on the shelf. Come to think of it, there were no marks on the shelf at all. It was laden with dust, and it hadn't been disturbed for years, not even by the dress." He shook his head in bewilderment. "What am I going to do?"

"If you like, I'll have Jim take a look at it," suggested Gertrude. "He'll charge you a fee, of course, but it'll be well worth it."

"What'll I tell Amanda? She'll think I've entirely flipped."

"Don't tell her anything. She's in the hospital and she

doesn't need to know about any of it. I happen to know that Jim's just finished a case. He'll probably be glad to take on another one right away. He truly loves his work, you know, and the whole thing can be over with before Amanda gets out of hospital."

"That quickly?" asked Alec.

"That quickly."

CHAPTER 11

"I've seen this house before." Mary Ann bounced in her excitement. She and Jim had just pulled to a stop on Rochford Square. "It's always had a kind of supernatural glow to it, even in the daytime. I've always wanted to know who lived here and what was going on in it."

"You're about to find out," said Jim. "C'mon Betsy, time to go hunting."

The big, shaggy dog woofed and pushed her way out of the back seat of the mini. She stood on the sidewalk for a moment, sniffed the air, and then took off at a dead gallop toward the back yard of Alec's house barking all the way.

"Hm," said Jim, "you don't suppose she's found something already?" They followed her to the back of the house where they found her barking wildly at the corner of the fence.

"Hush, now, Betsy, you'll wake the neighbours," said Jim. Betsy hushed, although she continued to whine and run in circles, not quite daring to investigate the back fence.

"Can you see what she's barking at, Mary Ann?"

Mary Ann peered into the dusk. "Not in the physical," she replied.

"What about in the astral?"

"Gimme a second and I'll try to see." She sat down on the ground and slowed her breathing, inducing a light trance. "Lights," she muttered softly. "Just lights. They're fading now." She released her trance state and sighed.

"Well?" asked Jim, as Betsy lay down at his feet with a great doggie whine.

Mary Ann scrambled to her feet. "Yuck, that ground's damp." She brushed the grass from the seat of her blue jeans. "I didn't see anything except a glow of light over in that left corner, and that might be anything from mineral glow to reflected light from somewhere."

"No ghostly figures?"

"Not even a trailing hanky." Mary Ann giggled.

"However, the glow faded when I looked at it steadily, so there might be something there. Maybe we'll have better luck after it gets darker. I'll have another look then."

"Betsy lost interest while you were in trance, so the energy field may just have faded. Let's go and see if Gertrude and Don have arrived yet."

Alec opened the door to the four ghost hunters. "Meow-ow," said Kitty, who twined herself around Gertrude's ankles.

"Where'd you come from?" asked Alec. "I thought I put you outside!"

"Oh, you mean the cat." Mary Ann giggled again. "I thought for a minute you meant us."

"Come in, come in," said Alec. "Indeed, I did mean the cat. It hasn't been but five minutes since I put her out the side door. You must be Mary Ann."

"Pleased to meet you," said Mary Ann, sticking out a plump mitt. "And your cat too. This is Jim MacDonald, my boss, so to speak."

"This is certainly a lovely house you've got here, Alec," said Jim. "It must be the envy of the neighbourhood."

"If they knew what's been happening here lately it

wouldn't be," said Alec. "I even think I'm hearing voices now."

"Oh? When did this begin?" asked Don, ever the psychologist.

"Just a few minutes ago when I put Kitty out. They seemed to come from the back yard. It gave me such a start I didn't even try to investigate."

"Maybe you should have." Mary Ann chuckled. "It was only us out there getting a feel for the ambiance."

"Now I feel silly," said Alec, "but so much has been happening here lately that I'm distrusting my senses."

"Happens to everyone in this situation," said Jim. "We need to get on with this investigation, if you can show us the layout of the house, please."

"Certainly, right this way." They toured the downstairs with Betsy leading the way snuffling into every corner she could reach. Kitty followed her at a respectful distance.

"Is this the only way to the upstairs?" asked Jim.

"No, there's a back staircase that goes up to the maid's room from the back porch. It enters the room which seems to be almost an extension of the landing of the main staircase, then it continues up to the attic. We never use it as it's not in very good condition."

"I'll need to see both of them, if you don't mind."

"Right this way, then." Alec led the group up the front stairs. Betsy bounded past them and stood barking and whining at the door to the maid's room, which stood slightly ajar. Kitty followed at a sedate pace, sniffed at the door, then pushed it open far enough to accommodate her whiskers and slid gracefully and silently into the room. Betsy tried to follow her, but only succeeded in closing the door on her.

"Well, I think we've found a 'hot spot,'" said Jim. "I haven't seen Betsy so excited since we deghosted that house out in Vernon River a few years ago."

"This's the room where Amanda saw the woman." Alec pushed open the door, and flipped on the light. "I found the baby dress on the floor right there. We wanted to use this room for the nursery, but I'm not so sure anymore. We haven't furnished it yet. Amanda wants to paper it in nursery paper first."

"Is this where the other stairs go down?" asked Mary Ann.

"Yes, they go down there to the porch, and they go up

here to the attic." Alec opened another door and pulled the string, flooding the stairwell to the attic with forty watts of brightness.

"Is there a light in the attic besides this one?" asked Jim.

"No, there's not. That's another job I mean to do, but haven't had time to yet. I wanted to put strip lighting up there. It's as dark as Egypt even in the daytime."

Jim lumbered up the stairs followed by Mary Ann and Betsy. "It is dark up here all right."

"Achoo!" Mary Ann sneezed loudly. "Dusty too!" She sniffed.

Betsy snuffled her way around the perimeter of the attic, pausing when she got to the place where Roderick had seen the pretty lady. "Woof?" she said.

"Another hot spot?" asked Jim.

"It might be," said Mary Ann. "Betsy's terribly interested in that area over there. I can't see anything, but I'll psych it out better later."

"C'mon, then Betsy, time to go downstairs," said Jim.

The big dog whined and came away from her investigations looking back over her shoulder frequently as she obeyed her master.

"These are the stairs to the back porch," said Alec, as Jim and Mary Ann rejoined the others in the maid's room. He pulled the light string, the light flared and went out. "Drat! That would go out just when we wanted to see down there. I'll just go and get another bulb for it."

A few minutes later light was restored. "Be careful on those steps," said Alec, "I don't know how sturdy they are any more. They'll hold my weight, but I don't know how much more."

Jim started down the stairs, which creaked loudly under his bulky person. Mary Ann followed carefully after him. Betsy woofed and pushed her way past both of them disappearing around the corner halfway down.

"Pst!!" exploded Kitty from the darkness somewhere below.

"Yipe!" said Betsy as she made a u-turn and pushed her way back past Jim and Mary Ann, a set of parallel red stripes decorating her nose.

"I guess we know who's boss around here," said Mary Ann.

"I think I've found how Kitty gets into the house," called Jim from the depths of the stairwell. He pushed on the door at the bottom. It opened into the back porch, as Alec had said it would. Kitty trotted demurely out, leaped up onto the window sill, and began washing her ears. Jim closed the door again and returned to the upstairs.

"Has she got a hole down there?" asked Alec, as Jim and Mary Ann emerged from the dimness of the back stairs.

"There's a loose panel on the bottom of the door. She just pushes it aside and squeezes through and then it swings back in place behind her."

"Well, that explains why when she appears in the house it always seems to be from up here. She must be able to get into the porch some way or other too. I'll have to check that out for cat holes as well, I guess. I'll put a nail in that panel tomorrow."

"Do you need to go to the hospital yet this evening?" asked Gertrude.

"No, I told Amanda that I might have to work late tonight, that way if I don't show up she won't be worrying about me not coming. And if I do, I can just say that I finished early."

"We need to finish our tour here," said Jim. "There can't be too much more to see."

Alec led the way through the remainder of the upstairs. "It's really a pretty basic old house," he said as they completed the tour. "No secret passages, no hidden rooms."

"Just weird things happening at night," said Don.

"What happens next, then?" asked Alec.

"We need to research the history of the house and the surrounding area," said Gertrude.

"I also want to interview you a little more for the finer details of the situation," said Jim.

"I don't know how much more I can tell you."

"If I ask the right questions you'll be surprised at what you know but hadn't thought to tell me. Right now I'd like to see the shelf where you left the baby dress."

Jim picked up his flashlight and Alec led the way downstairs.

"It's right here, behind the furnace. I don't know if you can get in here, it's an awfully tight squeeze, I can barely make it."

Jim stuck his head around the old converted coal furnace, but his large solid body wouldn't follow. He held his light high, attempting to see the surface of the shelf. "I guess I can't quite make it. Here Gertrude, you're a Skinny-Minny, you take a look."

Gertrude took the light from Jim and slid into the space behind the furnace. "Alec's right, there's been nothing on this shelf for years. Kitty's been back here though, I can see her paw marks in the loose dirt on the floor." She slid out of the small space after making a thorough inspection of the floor and walls and shelf. "There's nothing there at all except Kitty's footprints on the floor." She handed the flashlight back to Jim and brushed the cobwebs out of her hair.

"Well, I know I put that little dress on the shelf yesterday morning," said Alec. "There're no other shelves down here, so it had to be that one, unless I dreamed the whole thing. I was pretty tired by that time. Maybe I didn't find a baby dress at all."

"Oh, you probably did," said Mary Ann. "In a case of haunting all sorts of strange things occur."

Alec turned to lead the way upstairs. "So you think it really is a haunting?"

"We have no way of knowing for sure until we check out all the other possibilities," said Jim. "Mary Ann gets excited when she thinks she's on the trail of a ghost."

"Anyone for tea?" asked Alec, filling the kettle and setting it on the stove to heat. He began rummaging in the cupboard. "Amanda should have some cookies around here someplace."

"Tea sounds wonderful. Ghost hunting's thirsty work." Gertrude smoothed her red curls again.

"So Alec," asked Jim, when they had settled themselves around the kitchen table with cookies and tea, "what do you know about this house?"

"If you mean in terms of its history, not much. I only know that Aunt Martha deeded it to Amanda in her will. Amanda's her only close living relative, and kind of a favourite of hers over the years."

"Do you know how Martha may have acquired it?"

Alec shook his head. "Not really, but if memory serves me correctly, I think Amanda said one time that she came here as a bride. I don't know if it was in her husband's family or not. They didn't have any children, so she made a lot of Amanda when she was growing up."

"How was Amanda related to her?"

"Amanda was the daughter of Martha's youngest sister. There was a gap of about fifteen or so years between Martha and Mary, and Amanda was a late child too, so Martha was pretty old when Amanda came along. The women in Amanda's family weren't very fertile. Amanda's an only child, although there are lots of cousins on her father's side."

"When's Amanda due?" asked Gertrude.

"According to the calendar she's due just after the first of the year. They haven't done an ultrasound yet, unless they did it today."

"They'll probably do one soon, since she had that fall," said Gertrude. "They'll want to make sure the baby's okay."

"You don't happen to have the deed to this place handy, do you?" asked Jim.

"It's in the safety deposit box. I can get it for you tomorrow."

Jim shook his head. "Don't bother, I can research it through City Hall. I have to go there tomorrow anyway. Tell me again about this mist you saw. What were you doing when you saw it?"

"Well, Amanda and I had just finished doing the dishes. We were talking about what to name the baby. It was dusk and we hadn't yet pulled the curtains. I happened to look out, and I saw what I thought was a patch of fog, except it kind of gathered itself into a shape, and moved along the fence almost to the end, then passed through the pickets and disappeared."

"Did Amanda see it too?"

"Not that time, but when I told her what I'd just seen she said that she'd seen something similar one day when I was away to Halifax on a conference. It was the first time she'd spoken about it."

"What day was that?"

"I'll have to think. It was raining, I remember her telling me that. It must have been the day that she had her doctor's appointment. She was just coming home from that, I think. She didn't think anything of it at the time because it was raining."

"It was the next night that I came to visit with her," said Gertrude. "We heard crying that night. We searched the house over but couldn't find a thing. We'd just finished our tour when Kitty appeared again. Amanda said she hadn't let her in and I hadn't, so it was kind of a mystery how she got here."

"Not so much of a mystery any more," said Alec. "She'd found a hole in the foundation and had been sleeping in the cellar. It was behind that shrubbery down the driveway and I couldn't see it from the outside. I've plugged it since, though I still haven't found how she gets from the cellar to the upstairs."

"That loose panel in the door to the maid's room is how she's been getting up there, now all you have to do is find how she gets from the cellar to the porch," said Jim. "When else have you heard the crying?"

"I've only heard it a couple of times. Until now I've always just blamed it on the cats." He poured more tea into everyone's cup. "Oh, yes, and I did have a most peculiar dream when I was away. It was very real, although it was very simple. It had to do with babies crying and Amanda."

"Is that all?" asked Mary Ann.

"That's all. I never have very elaborate dreams."

"What was it about the dream that it's stayed with you?" asked Don.

Alec shrugged. "I don't really know. I guess it was more the tone than the content. It bothered me enough that I came home early."

"How was Amanda when you got home?" asked Gertrude.

"Nervous, I'd say, although she'd never admit to it. She had a dream just about the same time that I was having mine, and it frightened her. Frightened Kitty too, if what she said about it all was true."

"Hm," said Mary Ann, "if the cat reacted it might not have been a dream. Animals are usually quite perceptive."

"How long are they going to keep Amanda in the hospital?" asked Gertrude.

"I don't know for sure. I guess until they feel confident that she won't miscarry. I suppose they could send her home anytime."

"Well, here's the plan," said Jim. "Tomorrow I'll go to City Hall, and get whatever information is available on the ownership of this property. I have government survey maps so I'll see if there's anything geologically unstable in the area. I should be able to find out the history of this house from the archives. Can you get off work early tomorrow afternoon?"

"If nothing major happens I can. They owe me a lot of overtime that I'll probably never get unless I take it."

"Good. I'll meet you here about three o'clock, and we'll go over the basement inch by inch, and try to cat-proof it. Gertrude and Mary Ann can join us after supper and we'll get on with the actual ghost hunt."

CHAPTER 12

"This house used to belong to a big lawyer here in town," said Jim the next afternoon, as he and Alec were inspecting the cellar for cat holes.

"I didn't know that," said Alec. "When was that?"

"He built it for his bride in eighteen-ninety. I guess he was quite well off for a young fellow. His father was a businessman here, and he also had some interests in England, so none of them were hurting for cash."

"I wonder how old he was?"

"His birth was recorded in the newspaper as being in eighteen-sixty-five. I looked up his christening record in the Kirk archives and it corresponded closely with that, so I guess he was twenty-five when he got married. His wife was quite a bit younger than he was."

"Was she anyone?"

"I couldn't find out much about her. I don't think she was local. Whoever she was, she was well off. She brought a couple of servants with her: a cook and a lady's maid."

"Meow." Kitty jumped down from the coal chute startling both Jim and Alec.

"Kitty, how did you get in here?" asked Alec.

"Right through this hole." Jim shone his flashlight on the cover of the coal chute.

"I didn't know that hole was there," said Alec. "It certainly isn't visible from the outside."

"No, it probably isn't, it'll be right next to the hinges on the outside, and it'll look like part of the frame, I'll bet. I'll stick something through it from here so you can see where it is, and you go up and nail something over it on the outside. I'll keep looking for other places she might have gotten in."

"Out you go, Kitty, said Alec putting the little cat out the back door after supper. "You can come back when we're finished."

"Do you have to see Amanda this evening?" asked Jim.

"I told her I'd be there later," said Alec. "She's becoming very restless and wants to come home. They're doing an ultrasound on her tomorrow, so I expect she'll be home right after that."

"So we really only have tonight to solve this mystery," said Gertrude, who had arrived a few minutes earlier. "Mary Ann should be here any time now, I was just talking to her on the phone before we came over."

A car door slammed in the driveway, and a breathless Mary Ann was soon pounding on the porch door. "Kitty sure looks forlorn out there on the doorstep," she said when Alec had opened the door to her.

Alec laughed. "She's upset because Jim and I plugged all her cat holes this afternoon, and put her outside for the evening."

"Well, the sooner we get going, the sooner we get finished, and can let the poor beastie in again," said Mary Ann. "What d'you want want us to do first, Jim?"

"I want you and Gertrude to go around and seal all the windows and doors to the outside with thread, just like we always do. I want to make sure there's no one getting in from outside. Alec, this would be a good time for you to go and visit with Amanda. Once we seal the house you can't come in or go out until we've finished our survey. You're welcome to stay, of course, but you've either got to stay or go."

"I guess I'd better go, then." Alec shrugged into his sweater. "I'll be back after visiting hours."

"Call before you come, so we'll know to let you in," said Gertrude. "As a matter of fact, you could go and spend the evening with Don. He's home babysitting with Roderick, and'll probably be glad of the company."

"While I set up my equipment in the maid's room, you two can be psyching out the rooms down here. A half hour a room should do, since we're pretty sure we know where the 'hot spot' is. Work together, then we can be sure you're not just seeing things if you actually do see something. Don't fall asleep, Mary Ann."

"I won't." Mary Ann yawned an enormous yawn. "Where d'you want to start, Gertrude?"

"I guess, the living room, it seems to be the logical place. Shall we seal the rooms separately, or seal the house as a whole, Jim?"

"Both," said Jim absently. He was calibrating his machines.

Mary Ann shrugged. "Whatever you say, boss." She rolled her eyes at Gertrude. "Let's get on with it then."

"That seems like over-kill," Gertrude picked up the spool of black sewing thread.

A half hour of hard work saw the downstairs rooms sealed inside and out. "I wonder if we need to do the upstairs too?" Mary Ann collapsed on the sofa in the living room.

Gertrude made a face. "Let's make sure he's paying attention to what we're saying this time when we ask. I don't think we really needed to seal on the inside too. I'll go and ask him."

She was back in a few minutes. "No, he's sealed the doors into the maid's room from the stairs, and he's already checked the outside of the house for ways into it that a prankster might use. He's busy up there setting up his cameras and light meters and magnetometers and that other thing-um-a-jig he uses to identify power surges. He said to go ahead and begin trancing the rooms down here."

"Oh, good," said Mary Ann, "just what I was hired for.

Now I can have a rest." She propped her plump legs on the hassock and made herself comfortable.

"Now don't you go to sleep on me." Gertrude settled herself in the wing chair. "I don't want to be the only one seeing things."

"I won't." Mary Ann looked for all the world like she was already well on the way to slumber land.

I'll bet! thought Gertrude. Jim'll be shaking you awake in about thirty minutes. She propped herself more securely in her chair and began her breathing routine to induce trance. In a moment the room seemed to darken and change. Whispers of genteel conversations penetrated her awareness. A flutter of long skirts created a slight breeze as they passed. A faint outline of Alec and Amanda super-imposed itself briefly on Mary Ann where she sat on the sofa. In all aspects of the history of the living room, peace and calmness seemed to be the order.

Gertrude terminated her trance after fifteen minutes and roused Mary Ann. "Wakey, wakey, Mary Ann. Time to compare notes."

Mary Ann jumped. "Oh, sorry, I guess I did fall asleep. What did you see?"

"Not much, but then I didn't expect to see much here. It was just the usual overlap of people and events, none of it very clear or very exciting. People lived peacefully in this room, at least. Let's do the dining room next. Can you stay awake?"

Mary Ann laughed. "I've had my nap."

They proceeded through each of the downstairs rooms finding nothing untoward in any of them. "This has to be the dullest house we've ever psyched out," said Mary Ann to Jim when they had completed their task.

"Only four more rooms, and then you'll be able to do the maid's room and the attic," said Jim.

"D'you mean we have to do the bathroom too?"

"Every room, that's the only way we can be sure we're not missing anything."

Mary Ann sighed.

"Are you all set up in the maid's room yet?" asked Gertrude.

"Not quite. I will be when you guys are ready to trance it."

An hour later they gathered on the landing again. "What's the story on the upstairs?" asked Jim.

"Huh!" said Gertrude, "nothing. Not one single thing. Oh, we had a few whispers, and a rustle of fabric, and a few faint outlines of people moving around, but like I said, essentially nothing."

"Hm, that's strange, you should have at least seen Amanda in her distress the other night. From what Alec said, she was scared enough to have affected him in Halifax."

"We did see Amanda, but we didn't see what had frightened her, and none of the sound came through."

Jim shook his head. "That's very strange. I wonder if something's blocking us?"

"Maybe, said Mary Ann. "Remember that house over in Truro we did last year? We couldn't get anywhere with it until the daughter came home for the weekend, then all hell broke loose."

"Yes, but that was a poltergeist," said Jim. "She and the mother didn't get along and the energy they generated between them set that off. I don't think that's what's happening here."

"I don't either," said Gertrude. "I don't get the feeling of excess energy anywhere here. It's all very peaceful and calm. I even saw Aunt Martha knitting in the kitchen in the rocking chair."

"Well, let's get on with the maid's room, and see if it's

as hot as we think it is," said Mary Ann.

A half hour later Gertrude and Mary Ann emerged from the room, two very puzzled psychics. "There's nothing there either," they said in unison.

"What do you mean, there's nothing there." Jim frowned. "There can't be nothing there."

"There's not a ripple on the ether! Nothing, just nothing!" said Mary Ann.

"I don't understand it," said Gertrude. "With what Amanda said she saw in here, and Alec finding the disappearing baby dress, there has to be something here. We'll try the attic."

A psychic assessment of the attic revealed nothing as well. The three ghost hunters sat on the top steps of the main staircase and tried to puzzle the problem out.

"What do we do now?" asked Gertrude. "There's not even a clue as to what's going on here."

"Maybe that's the answer." Mary Ann leaned her chin on her chubby hands. "Maybe there really isn't anything going on at all."

"But Alec and Amanda wouldn't perpetrate a hoax," said Gertrude. "What reason would they have for doing that?"

"Heaven knows why anybody does anything. Besides it might just be hormones."

"I don't think so. This is not pickles and ice cream, you know. Besides, whatever she saw frightened her badly enough to cause her to fall downstairs."

Mary Ann sighed. "I guess you're right. She wants this baby too much to do anything to hurt it, if what Alec says is true."

"Which brings us back to the point you ladies made earlier, something may be blocking us," said Jim.

"Mm," said Gertrude, "but what?"

"I wonder if it's not so much blocking us, as that it may not have enough energy of its own to reveal itself to us?" Mary Ann pursed her lips. "Maybe it can't draw on our energy to manifest itself."

"Perhaps, but how many ghosts have we met that couldn't draw on our power?"

"That one over in Newfoundland last winter. Remember us sitting out that raging snowstorm waiting for the stupid ghost to appear and all it could do was weep and moan."

"Yeah, we never did find out what it wanted, did we?" said Gertrude. "It was easy to appease, though."

"I felt kind of silly, sitting in that dark old kitchen chanting prayers for the dead," said Jim. "I was sure glad when they finally restored the power and the lights came on."

"I wonder if that's what's going on here? Maybe the ghost just doesn't know how to access our psychic power and can't appear."

"It did all right the other night when Amanda saw it," said Mary Ann.

"Maybe Amanda's the answer," said Jim. "After all, it is her house, and she has a lot of emotion and memories invested here. Maybe that's what the ghost's drawing on."

"If that's the case then there's not much we can do here until she comes home." Gertrude yawned.

Mary Ann straightened and stretched. "Well, I'm for home and bed, if there's nothing we can do here tonight."

"D'you mean you haven't had enough sleep this evening?" Gertrude quirked an eyebrow at her.

"I think I'll seal this room, and leave all the equipment up and running, and see what we have in the morning," said Jim. "Send Alec back here when you get home, will you, Gertrude? I want to talk to him."

❖

"Gertrude tells me you didn't find anything," said Alec as he closed the front door behind himself.

"Just the usual psychic noise that a house collects over the years," replied Jim. "C'mon upstairs, I want to show you something." Jim made his way to the second floor again, and opened the door to the maid's room. "I've left all this equipment set up and running for the night. I'm going to seal this room and see what we get in the morning."

"That's quite an impressive array of machines," said Alec. "What're they all for?"

"They measure different things, like heat, air pressure, magnetic forces, power surges, things like that. I have the camera set to take photos if anything alive or dead should pass into the room. They're sensitive enough to be disturbed by anything on this floor, so if you get up to go to the bathroom during the night I want you to take note of the time so I can eliminate that from the records."

"I could sleep downstairs," said Alec.

"Perhaps that would be best, but you still need to take note of the times you're moving around in case they do pick up anything."

"Sure thing," said Alec. "Do you have time for a cup of

tea? I was just going to put the kettle on."

"Tea sounds fine." Jim followed him into the kitchen. "You know, this could still be a prankster." Jim stared hard at Alec. "I wouldn't like to think that I've wasted all my good time and effort on a case that was nothing but a game." He settled his bulk at the kitchen table still looking at Alec.

Alec blushed under the pressure of his intense stare. "I hope you don't think I set this whole thing up. I wouldn't do such a thing! Amanda's in the hospital hurting because of this whole business, and we could have lost our baby! If I had been creating a prank don't you think I'd have stopped by now?"

"Sorry Alec, I had to make sure," said Jim. "You'll never know how many people think it's a great joke to pretend there's a ghost in the house, and they'll stop at very little to carry it all through. I don't know you very well, I only have Trudy's word that you are what you appear to be."

The kettle shrilled into the long silence that followed. Alec rose from his chair to make the tea. "I'm sorry I've come across as so shallow," he said at last.

"You don't, but it's just as I said, I can never be too careful about people and their private agendas. You see,

I'm not a sensitive like Gertrude and Mary Ann, so I have to rely on what I can observe with my two physical eyes, and sometimes that means I have to be very blunt. Look at it this way, I wouldn't be leaving a whole roomful of very expensive equipment in your care if I didn't have some regard for you."

Alec's face lost some of its strained look. "Well, I'm glad for that. You know I'd never do anything to hurt Amanda." He got up to pour the tea into mugs, weariness in his every movement. "She's my life."

"I'm glad you're home." Don cuddled Gertrude close in the front hall. "Roderick was just beside himself this evening. I don't know what got into him."

"What was he up to?" She snuggled closer.

"He was very agitated all evening, and he wouldn't go to bed. I finally threatened him with a spanking, and all he did was say that if that's what I needed to do, that I should do it."

Gertrude laughed. "Spoken like the son of a psychologist! He knew you wouldn't do it."

Don sighed. "And the rascal was right, too."

Gertrude released herself from Don's embrace and turned toward the kitchen. "I could use a cuppa, how about you?"

"Sure, I'll just go and check on our offspring."

Don returned a few minutes later. "You know, he still hasn't gone to sleep. He's up there talking to himself. I can't tell if it's Paulie or the pretty lady who's visiting tonight."

"What was he going on about this evening?"

"He was very upset about you being out on a case."

"But he's never bothered about what I'm doing before." Gertrude set out cups and saucers. "Want some cinnamon toast?"

"Please," said Don. "He wouldn't leave Alec alone either. It was like he knew where you were and what was going on and he didn't like it. He kept talking about the pretty lady too."

"He could very well have known where I went. He is a sensitive too, you know."

Don made a face. "I'm trying to not think about that aspect of our son's growth and development."

Gertrude shook her head. "It's not going to do a bit of good to block it." She set a plate of toast in front of him.

"I know, I just keep hoping it'll go away."

"It won't," said Gertrude.

Roderick's scream of terror suddenly echoed through the house.

Gertrude and Don seemed to reach Roderick's bedside in seconds. Gertrude scooped him into her arms and tried to rock him. He fought her, a blank look of horror reflected in his blue eyes. His breath caught in his throat as he inhaled for another scream. "Roddy, Roddy, wake up. Everything's all right. Mommy's here."

Don stood helplessly by while Gertrude tried to calm their son. "It must have been a nightmare," he said. "Children of that age get them frequently." He sat down on the bed. "I'm not surprised he had one tonight, he was that wound up earlier," he said above Roderick's wails.

"Let's take him downstairs," said Gertrude. "Maybe he'll quiet better in bright light." She handed the thrashing child over to Don, and led the way out of the room. Roderick's screams lessened somewhat as they carried him into the kitchen.

Don sat down in the rocking chair with him and began to rock. "There, there, now," he soothed, "you're okay."

Roderick's sobs quieted and he seemed to come to himself. He lay still in his father's arms and looked around. "How'd I get here?" he asked.

"We carried you," said Gertrude. "You had a bad dream."

"Wasn't a dream." Roderick recovered some of his self-assurance. "It was real."

"Honey, you were sound asleep. You just woke up now."

"It wasn't a dream," said Roderick.

"How do you know it wasn't a dream?" Don sat Roderick upright on his lap.

"Because I was there."

"It only seemed as if you were there. Dreams can be like that."

"What was the dream about?" asked Gertrude.

"The pretty lady put her hand over my face and I couldn't breathe. I thought she was my friend." Roderick started to cry again.

"That certainly would be a scary thing to have happen," said Don, "but it was only a dream."

"It wasn't a dream." Roderick began to sob again.

"Maybe you shouldn't be encouraging the pretty lady to talk with you before you go to sleep," suggested Gertrude.

Roderick hiccoughed. "I don't, she just comes."

Gertrude wiped the unhappy little face. She turned his face to the light to do so and stifled a gasp. The faint blue of finger marks was beginning to show around his mouth and nose. She silently pointed them out to Don. To Roderick she said, "It's okay, honey. It's all over now. I'll say a prayer of protection for you when you go back to bed, and she won't be able to hurt you again."

Don rocked his small son until he fell into a gentle sleep, then he carried him back to his bed, and stood looking down at him while Gertrude prayed over him. He's so like Gertrude, thought Don. I hope this psychic business doesn't harm him. I feel so helpless!

CHAPTER 13

So what did you find?" asked Mary Ann the next evening, as they settled themselves around Gertrude's kitchen table.

"Nothing," said Jim. "Not one thing. I don't think there was even a draft in that room all night."

"Your equipment all checked out?" asked Gertrude.

"Oh, yes. I checked it before I left home, and then again when I set it up. Everything was working fine."

"Did Alec stay in the house last night?" asked Mary Ann.

"He slept downstairs."

"Is he trustworthy?"

"He's the Rock of Gibraltar personified," said Gertrude.

Her colour and her voice rose in defence of Alec. "I've known him all my life, and I've never known him to do anything underhanded."

"So have I, for that matter," said Don more calmly.

"Okay, okay," said Jim. He laughed. "We get the message. Besides I warned him last night about hoaxes, and I'm pretty sure that he wouldn't do anything like that, especially if it puts Amanda in danger."

"Speaking of Amanda," said Gertrude, "she came home this afternoon."

"How is she?" asked Mary Ann.

"Right as rain again. I don't know how she'll take it when she finds out about us, though."

"You mean Alec hasn't told her yet?" asked Jim. "But we're due over there in half an hour to continue our search."

"If she doesn't have hysterics over it all, and have to be re-admitted to the Queen Elizabeth, she may be able to encourage some of those ghosties to come out and play." Mary Ann chuckled.

"The pretty lady hurted me," said Roderick from his place on the floor where he had been quietly pushing his trucks down imaginary roads and talking to Paulie. "She didn't want me to cry."

"What's he talking about?" asked Jim.

"Oh, he just had a bad dream last night," said Gertrude. "He said the pretty lady tried to smother him."

"Humph!" said Don. "Some dream! You can see the fingerprints around his mouth."

"By golly, so you can." Mary Ann inspected Roderick's face more closely. "Didn't he meet the pretty lady over at Amanda's?"

"Indeed he did," said Don, "and I wish she'd stayed over there."

"Maybe that's the reason you didn't get anything on your charts last night." Mary Ann giggled. "Maybe the pretty lady's behind it all and she wasn't home."

"Don't be silly," said Jim. "I don't think it was that at all. I think it was because Amanda wasn't home."

"You mean you think she's triggering all this?" asked Gertrude.

"I wouldn't be surprised," said Jim. "If you'll think about it for a few minutes, there hasn't been any activity in that house since the night she went to the hospital."

"You're right," said Gertrude. "She may very well be

triggering it. I wonder why her though?"

"Beats me." Jim shrugged, "but we're going to find out." He looked at his watch. "It's time to go ghost hunting."

"It's so nice to see you looking so fit." Gertrude greeted Amanda when they arrived at her house a few minutes later.

"I'm fine, and the baby's fine," said Amanda without even a trace of a smile.

Oh, oh, thought Gertrude, Alec's told her what's been going on and she's not happy about it. I wonder if they know that I'm a psychic? I wonder if it'll make any difference? "These are some colleagues of mine." She ignored Amanda's coolness. "My boss Jim, and his assistant, Mary Ann."

"How do you do?" said Amanda. "Won't you come in?"

"Alec's told you about our work here?" Gertrude approached the subject head on.

"Yes, he has, and I think you're barking up the wrong tree," she said. Her tone was prim. "There are no such things as ghosts."

"Unfortunately there are sometimes such things as

ghosts, and they can create quite a bit of havoc in the physical when they want to," said Jim. "From the lack of activity in this house while you were away, I'd say you were probably triggering the phenomenon here."

Amanda paled. "You're joking! This is Aunt Martha's house and she'd never allow such things as ghosts!"

"I don't think Aunt Martha has too much to say about it," said Gertrude. "As I remember, she was a peaceful old lady who didn't stand for much nonsense. She always did the appropriate thing and probably went to her reward without even a backward glance."

Amanda smiled slightly at this description. "That was Aunt Martha all right. I still miss her." She lapsed into a troubled silence and sat staring for some minutes at her hands, folded tightly in her lap. "Why me?" she finally wailed.

"That's what we'd like to know too," said Gertrude gently, "and with your help, I think we can find out."

"Oh, do you think so?" Amanda brightened considerably at this news. "What do I need to do?"

"Just do whatever you normally do, pretend that we're not even here."

"But how can I do that? I can't very well ignore you."

"No, what I meant was that you should have your meals at the usual time, and go to bed at your usual time, and get up at your usual time, just as if we weren't here. We'll be checking a variety of things pertinent to the investigation and generally trying to keep quiet at night."

"You're going to stay all night? I'll have to get beds ready, and I haven't even checked the pantry since I came home." She started to rise from her seat.

"Don't worry about any of that," said Jim. "We're going to be sitting up on your landing all night. The only thing you have to do is show me where you keep the coffee."

"Oh," said Amanda, somewhat deflated. "It's in the fridge, and the filters are in the canister on the counter. The pot's on the counter too. Would you like some now?"

"In a while will be fine," said Jim. "In the meantime, I'm going to go and check my equipment, and make sure everything's in working order. I'll need some help, Mary Ann."

"Oh, Trudy, why didn't you tell me?" asked Amanda in distress, after Jim and Mary Ann had left.

"Because I was afraid you wouldn't want to be friends

anymore. I thought it would be a repeat of school. I thought you'd think I was crazy, like they always said my mother was. I thought all kinds of things."

"We're not children any more," said Amanda. Her tone was gentle. "I would have worked through it. I need a friend too, you know."

Gertrude blushed. "I'm sorry, Amanda. It's just that I had to live with what my mother portrayed herself to be, and it was very lonely. I rarely tell anyone that I have the gift. My mother liked to think she had it, but hers wasn't nearly the strength of mine. All she could do was tell fortunes, and some of that she made up. I don't trust very many people with my secret, because most people don't understand, and it makes them nervous and afraid of me. They think I can read minds and do parlour tricks."

"And can you? Read minds, I mean."

"Yes, but it's not worth the effort it would take to do it. I'd have to go into a light trance in order to gain the concentration necessary to 'read,' and most people aren't thinking anything worth reading anyway."

"What about the parlour tricks?"

"Those aren't worth the effort either. I'm a working

psychic, I don't waste my energy on frivolous things."

"What about Roderick? Is he psychic too? Was that what was happening when he saw the pretty lady in the attic?"

Gertrude sighed. "I'm afraid he is. Don's not too pleased about it, he has trouble enough dealing with my gift. Roddy's started very early, and I wonder what he'll do with it. My gift stayed latent until about five years ago. That's how I met Don again. I thought I was losing my mind, and I went for counselling, not realizing that Dr. Donald Harvey, PhD, was Don Harvey, the hockey star."

"That must have been a shock." Amanda laughed. "I remember what he was like in high school."

"What who was like in high school?" Alec brought in a tray of tea cups and the teapot. "I made you ladies some tea. You've been doing so much talking in here I figured you'd be pretty dry by now."

"We were just talking about Don in high school." Amanda shifted her legs so that Alec could sit beside her.

"Oh, yeah, the jock hockey star of Charlottetown Rural. That was quite a cover. I wonder if Ian Alexander'll play hockey?"

Amanda shuddered. "I hope not. I don't want him to

come home with missing teeth and broken limbs."

"You're having a boy?" asked Gertrude.

"I don't know. I told them at the ultrasound today that I didn't want to know, so they didn't tell me."

"Well, maybe I wanted to know," said Alec. "It's my baby too." Just then a familiar cry echoed through the house.

Amanda jumped and laughed nervously. "It's starting early. It usually doesn't start until after dark."

Gertrude looked outside. "Well it's nearly that now. I'd like to have a look at your garden. It was about this time in the evening that you saw the mist, wasn't it?"

"Just about," said Alec. "You don't need to come if you don't want to, Amanda. Just rest here and think happy thoughts about our baby." Again the thin cry of a child in distress disturbed the air.

"It sounds hungry," said Amanda sadly. "I wish I could give it something to eat."

"Well, you can't until we find it." Gertrude rose from her chair to follow Alec. "And probably not even then."

"I sure hope all this doesn't affect our child." Alec led the way to the kitchen.

"I hope not either." Gertrude thought of the faint bruises

around Roderick's mouth. "If we can find out what's causing this and send it on its way, you shouldn't have any more trouble."

Alec drew back the kitchen curtains and looked out into the back yard. "There's nothing there now. Shall I keep watch for awhile?"

"Only if you want to," said Gertrude. "By the time we'd get here to have a look if you did see anything, it'd probably be gone. Amanda likely needs you worse than we need to see a mist in the garden."

Alec let the curtain fall back into place. "You're probably right. It doesn't take very long for it to form and dissipate, and Amanda does need me right now, she was pretty upset when I told her what we were doing."

"I hope she'll be able to sleep tonight, I suspect that the ghosties walk better when she's asleep."

By eleven thirty that night the house had quieted. Alec and Amanda had gone to bed, and the ghost hunters had arranged themselves on the landing outside the maid's room, with only the faint glow from the street lamps outside to light their surroundings. Their voices were subdued.

"I wonder what we'll see tonight," whispered Mary Ann.

"I don't know," said Gertrude, "but I have a feeling that it'll be good. I can feel the energy building."

"So I guess I was right," said Jim. "It is Amanda who's triggering this."

"It would seem so," whispered Gertrude. "Now be quiet for a few minutes, I want to try and get a fix on the energy."

"I'll go with you," said Mary Ann, and the two psychics lapsed into trance.

Together they surveyed the maid's room and the attic in their minds. The shadows seemed deeper than usual in the maid's room but they could not discern any strange forms.

"It's too soon," whispered Mary Ann in Gertrude's mind.

"We might as well go back," said Gertrude.

The night wore on in silence. The energy continued to grow until Gertrude felt like screaming with the pressure of it.

At three thirty Amanda stirred. Her dream had had a sense of distress and urgency about it. She couldn't quite remember the content. She lay there thinking about Alec and her baby and hoping that the ghost would soon be laid to its proper rest. I hope this never happens again, she thought. I guess I'm lucky, though, poor Gertrude has to live with this every day, especially since Roderick is psychic too. I wonder if he'll come over and play with our baby when it gets old enough? She began imagining the two children playing together in the yard, and dropped into a light sleep again. Something called to her in her dream. She got out of bed, put on her robe, and padded barefoot to the door.

"Must be someone getting up to the bathroom," whispered Mary Ann.

"It's Amanda," said Gertrude, "and she's not going to the bathroom, she's coming this way." They observed Amanda walking down the hall towards them.

"Is she sleep-walking?" asked Mary Ann.

"I believe she is," said Gertrude softly. "We'll have to be careful not to wake her too abruptly, we might frighten her."

"We're not going to waken her at all," said Jim quietly, as Amanda turned to enter the maid's room. "I just hope she doesn't trip on anything in there."

Amanda stopped with her hand on the door handle for a moment. "My baby," she muttered as the familiar sound of a crying baby floated on the early morning air. "She wants my baby."

A glow seemed to emanate from the open doorway. but the others couldn't see into the room from their place on the landing. Amanda backed up and screamed. "NO!" The light took form and came into the hallway, a woman in long skirts reached for Amanda. "NO!" Amanda screamed again. The light faded.

Alec came running and gathered Amanda into his arms. "Hush, hush, darling," he soothed her, "everything's going to be all right. I'm here now." He stroked her hair and rocked her gently as her sobs quieted.

Presently she became aware of her surroundings and stirred in his arms. "What am I doing out here?" she asked in a tiny voice. "I'm cold."

"Let's get you back to bed." Alec guided her gently down the hallway. In a few minutes he was back. "She's sleeping again. What happened out here? I didn't even know she was gone until I heard her scream. It was just like the other night when she fell."

"She appeared to be sleep-walking," said Jim. "Does she have a history of that?"

"Not that I know about," said Alec. "I'm sure she would have told me sometime or other, I've known her since we were children."

"Was she awake when you put her to bed?"

"She appeared to be. She was talking to me and making sense."

"Did she tell you what happened here?"

"She was pretty upset, but she did say that she had another dream about the woman and the baby. What did she say out here?"

Jim looked gravely at Alec. "She said, 'she wants my baby.'"

Alec stood staring at Jim in a stunned silence for a moment. "That's it! That's just it! We're moving out of here in the morning. What time is it anyway?"

Gertrude looked at her watch. "It's after four, almost dawn."

"You're up early," said Gertrude. She was attempting to creep into the house at five-thirty that morning but Don was already up and dressed.

"Humph! Up early! I haven't been to bed."

"Why not?"

"Roderick had nightmares all night. I'd just get him settled and back to sleep, when he'd wake up screaming again. I finally took him into bed with me, but he kicked and twitched so, that I couldn't go to sleep."

"Did that stop the nightmares?"

"I don't think so. He didn't scream anymore, but he sure was restless. I just put the kettle on." He turned and shuffled tiredly to the kitchen.

A sleepy Roderick appeared at the top of the stairs rubbing his eyes with a small fist. "Mommy! You're home!" He flew down the stairs and leaped into Gertrude's arms from the third step from the bottom. "I was so worried about you."

"You were?" said Gertrude in surprise. "Why were you worried about me?"

Roderick thought for a moment. "I don't know," he said finally. "I dreamed about the pretty lady last night. She's very frightened. She wants me to go with her, but I told her I didn't want to, that you were my Mommy now and that you'd miss me if I went with her."

"You bet I'd miss you." Gertrude kissed on his warm round cheek. "I want you here with me for a long time. Let's go and see what Daddy's doing in the kitchen."

CHAPTER 14

"I am not leaving my home." Amanda was vehement the next morning. "I will not let a dead woman drive me from this house!" The 'discussion' had been going on for some minutes.

"But Amanda," said Alec, "what if she intends to harm you or our baby?"

"She can't," said Amanda, "she's not real."

"But she almost did already."

"That was my own fault, I wasn't watching where I was going. Besides, Gertrude and the others need me here in order to make the ghost come out. If I'm not here she won't appear, and we'll never be able to get rid of her, and we'll never be able to live in this house again."

Alec gave in with a deep worried sigh. "Okay, I suppose you're right, but I don't know what I'll do if anything happens to you or our baby. I don't think I'll be able to forgive myself."

Or me, either, thought Amanda. "Where's Kitty? I haven't seen her since I came home."

"We put her out night before last when we were sealing the house, and she hasn't been back since. I think she was insulted."

"I hope she's not lost, or run away. I think I'll look for her after breakfast."

"I'm going out to Mary Ann's this morning for awhile," said Gertrude two days later. It had taken both her and Roddy a long day of naps and rest to recover from the previous night. She buttered toast for Roderick. "I think it's time we had a talk with Molly to see if she and Lucy can throw any light on our problem."

"Will you take Roderick with you?" Don poured milk on his cereal.

"Can I go too? Please Mommy," said Roderick. "I like it

at Aunt Mary Ann's, she has lots of cats, and maybe there'll be some new kittens."

"I doubt I could get a baby sitter on such short notice," said Gertrude. "Besides I think it's about time I introduced him to Molly and Lucy."

"Can't that wait for a few more years? After all, he is barely four."

Gertrude shook her head. "I don't think so. I've been thinking a lot about what happened the other night with the pretty lady, and I don't like what she did to him. I don't think I can protect him adequately from that kind of attack. I can't be with him night and day like a spirit can, and he's much too precocious to be left without a spiritual guardian anymore. I'd like to ask Molly to find us a suitable one."

"I see," said Don. "More spirits."

"I'm sorry I've brought you all this," said Gertrude sadly. "I'd change it if I could."

Don rose from his place at the table and put his arms around Gertrude. "I know you would, honey, but you can't, and anyway it's what makes you unique." He kissed the top of her red curls. "I'm getting used to it. It's just very frightening to have Roderick threatened and not be able to protect him myself. I have to depend on spirits that I can't even see, and I only have your word for the reality of their presence."

"Well, you'd have to anyway," Gertrude pointed out. "Isn't that what religion's all about? Believing in something you can't see?"

"But you see more than I do," said Don.

"I see an alternate reality, but I don't see God any better than you do. He's infinitely larger than any of us, including Molly and her pals. He permeates everything and everyone regardless of their beliefs or level of understanding, and I have to take Him on faith just as much as anyone else."

"Is that why you can perform as a psychic during the week, and go happily off to church on Sunday?"

"I have to take time to honour and worship my spiritual source. God gave me this gift and I have to take care of it and replenish it or it'll dry up on me, and I won't have it anymore."

"Hm," said Don, "I hadn't thought about it like that before." He returned to his place at the table and sat lost in thought for several minutes. "So you're saying that if

Molly and Lucy fix Roddy up with a guardian, we can be pretty sure that what happened the other night won't happen again."

Gertrude nodded. "Pretty sure."

Don was silent again. Presently he said, "I feel kind of silly asking this, but do I have a guardian?"

"Everyone has a guardian, sometimes more than one. You actually have two."

Don looked alarmed. "Am I in that much danger?"

"Being married to me creates its own brand of danger, and when you need protection it sometimes takes two."

"Are Molly and Lucy your guardians?"

"No, they're my colleagues, although sometimes they perform that service too. As a practising psychic, I have a whole crowd of guardians. Usually there are six just hanging around, but when I'm on a case, like this one, for instance, they call in all kinds of extra help."

"Well, I'm relieved to hear that." Don released the breath that he didn't know he'd been holding. "If you're going to be staying with Mary Ann for lunch, I'll eat downtown."

❖

"C'mon in." Mary Ann giggled as always. "You'll have to excuse the mess, I was up half the night with Sarah. She had her kittens last night. D'you want to see some new kittens, Roddy? They don't even have their eyes open yet."

"Oh, can I, Mommy?" Roderick danced from foot to foot in his excitement.

"Yes, you may, but only look, don't touch. Sarah's probably still a little nervous and she might scratch you if you get too close."

"They're here, behind the stove," said Mary Ann, "be very quiet."

Roderick peeked into the box containing the kittens, a look of awe coming over his little boy face. "O-oh, they're so tiny," he whispered. "They don't look like Sarah."

"Well, Sarah's a grown up cat, that's why," said Mary Ann. "Sarah's ears stand up from her head and she has long legs, and a long tail. If you be very quiet, you can sit here and watch them while I visit with your Mom. Would you like that?"

Roderick's eyes shone with delight. "Yes, please, Aunt Mary Ann. I'll be very good."

"I just made a pot of coffee, would you like some,

Gertrude? I made it strong, I could hardly keep my eyes open this morning." She poured coffee into two mugs, and passed one to Gertrude. "I expect you've already had breakfast."

"Ages ago." Gertrude laughed. "Don leaves for the office about seven-thirty every morning, so we get up quite early."

"Why does he leave that early?" asked Mary Ann around a mouthful of sweet roll.

"He likes to have an hour of peace and quiet so he can get administrative things done before he sees his first client. He has back to back appointments almost all day."

"Have you talked to Molly lately?"

"No, I haven't had time. I thought we might do that today. It's time we found a real guardian for Roderick. I don't like what happened to him the other night, and night before last he kept Don awake all night with his nightmares."

"You mean while we were working at Amanda's?"

"Yes, apparently the pretty lady spent the entire night trying to persuade him to go with her."

"It couldn't have been the entire night," said Mary Ann. "She was over there with us for at least part of the time."

"Well, Don did get him quieted down about three o'clock, he said, although he was still pretty restless. He was one tired little boy all day yesterday, and he was sure glad to see me in the morning. He said he was worried about me, whatever he meant by that."

"Why don't you talk to Molly, and see if she knows anything," suggested Mary Ann. "I'll keep an eye on Roderick."

"Thanks," said Gertrude. "I haven't had time to do this, we've been so busy over at Amanda's." She settled herself more comfortably in her chair and closed her eyes.

"It's about time you got here." Molly was in her usual place on the mantel shelf and in a bad mood too. "I've been calling you for two days."

"Sorry," said Gertrude, "I guess I just didn't hear you. I've been really worried about Roderick and the pretty lady. She bruised him the other night, and she's been pestering him to go with her."

"I know all that," said Molly a little more gently. "I was there."

"And you didn't try to stop her?"

"Oh, I tried, but she's very determined. It was all I could do to keep her from doing worse."

Gertrude frowned. "I don't like the sound of that. Who is she?"

"Her name's Prudence, she calls herself Pru a lot of the time. Other than that I can't tell you much."

"Can't or won't?" asked Gertrude.

"Can't," said Molly. "I haven't had time to do any research on her."

"What've you been doing?"

"Looking after your son," said Molly. "I can't do everything, you know, and I'm not supposed to be a guardian."

"Sorry," said Gertrude. "I guess I'm more than a little worried about this situation. I don't like it that the pretty lady has come to our house. I've never had that happen before."

"She followed Roderick home," said Molly. "There was nothing you could do about it."

Gertrude sighed. "I guess it's already time to get him some guardians. He's awfully young to need them but if he does, I guess he'd better have them."

"I've already attended to that," replied Molly. "I sent Lucy and Larry off to interview some candidates yesterday. C'mon in, guys. This is Roderick's mother, Gertrude.

Gertrude, this is Eddy, Larry's younger brother sometimes, and this is Freddy, Eddy's best friend."

"Pleased to meet you, mother," they replied in unison. "Where's our charge?"

"Over there," said Gertrude, "talking to the cat." She pointed mentally toward the stove where Roderick sat talking to Sarah in whispers.

"Kind of little to need protection, isn't he?" asked Eddy.

"He'll be turning four soon," said Molly, "and he's already sensitive. Besides he's extremely intelligent."

"So our work's cut out for us," said Freddy.

"You could say that," said Molly.

"I already did," said Freddy.

"Nice to have met you, mother," said Eddy. "We'll take good care of your child." The two spirits disappeared from Gertrude's consciousness, and took up their stations beside Roderick.

"They're kind of young, aren't they?" asked Gertrude.

"They're very old spirits," said Molly. "They're older than we are."

"That doesn't mean too much to me, since I have no idea how old I am in spiritual terms."

"That's because you're not supposed to know," said Molly. Her tone was snappish. "If that's all the business you have with me today, I have to go."

"Can you find out who Prudence was in that house?" called Gertrude after the rapidly fading Molly.

"I'll try," called Molly from far away.

CHAPTER 15

I spent the afternoon in the archives," said Jim, as he checked his equipment at Amanda's house that evening. "I finally found a household account book of that lawyer I told you about, Alec."

"That was a lucky find," said Alec. "Those things usually get thrown out. What was in it?"

"Mostly money transactions, but the names of the members of the household were there too."

"Was one of the names Prudence?" Gertrude checked the seals on the windows.

"Yes, how did you know?"

"I was talking to Molly this morning at Mary Ann's, and

she told me. Did the book give her last name?"

"Harrison," replied Jim. "She came to the Island with her mistress, I think. There was a largish sum of money paid out to her that summer for travel expenses to Boston. It didn't say why a servant would be travelling to Boston by herself, so I'm assuming she had some family business to attend to, and that Mrs. Archibald allowed her to go."

"Mrs. Archibald must have been from Boston, then, if her servant came from Boston," said Alec. "You did tell me that she brought her servant with her, didn't you?"

"Yes, she brought a cook and a maid with her when she got married. Again, I'm assuming because it doesn't say, but I think it's the same one, because the account book is dated the year after her marriage to Mr. Archibald."

"I guess that's a fairly safe assumption," said Alec. "People liked to hold onto good servants, and she must have been good, or she wouldn't have taken her with her in the first place. It was a long trip from Boston by boat. Was there any record of her being back here after that?"

"None that I could see, but the book only covered that one year."

"I wonder if she was sent home in disgrace?" said

Gertrude. "Maybe she did something terrible here and they sent her packing."

"Made off with the family silver?" Mary Ann chuckled.

"I somehow don't think so, for the same reason that she was here in the first place, she was a good servant." Gertrude pulled off another length of black thread.

"By the way, and changing the subject," said Alec, "I cleared out the back fence today."

"Why today, all of a sudden?" asked Gertrude.

Alec looked uncomfortable. "I saw the mist again this morning. I didn't tell Amanda, and she was still in bed, so she didn't see it."

"Was it the same as before?" Jim straightened up from his task.

"It did exactly the same thing as before, only the mist seemed to be much denser."

"Hm," said Jim, "I wonder if we're coming to a climax here at last? What did you do?"

Alec shrugged. "Nothing right then, but I spent this morning clearing out all the bushes and weeds that had accumulated over the years."

"Did you find anything?" asked Mary Ann.

"Not much," said Alec. "The ground was pretty rough back there. It looked as if there might have been a small building in that corner at one time. There's a faint outline in the ground."

"I wonder what that was?" said Gertrude.

"An outhouse?" said Mary Ann.

"I don't think so," said Alec. "This house has had indoor plumbing since the beginning, and the plumbing's all original."

"Maybe a tool shed?"

"I don't think that either, it was too small a building for that."

"Tea's ready if you guys are," called Amanda from downstairs.

"Just in time," said Jim, "I'm finished here."

They all made their way downstairs.

"Oh, Gertrude, Don said he's bringing Roderick over in a few minutes." Amanda filled the cups. "He just called and said that he's been giving him fits ever since you left, and he can't get him quieted down to go to bed."

"I don't know what's gotten into that child these last few weeks, but it's getting steadily worse. He's been having nightmares every night, and all he can talk about in the daytime is the pretty lady."

"His imagination's got the better of him, has it?" said Amanda.

"I don't think so," said Gertrude. "She bruised him the other day. I'm really kind of worried about it. I got Molly to hire a couple of guardians for him on the other side today. I just hope they're up to the task."

"Who's Molly?" asked Amanda.

"A colleague of mine," said Gertrude.

"A familiar spirit?"

"Yes," said Gertrude, "you could say that's what she is."

"Oh," said Amanda, a little surprised. "I never thought of that aspect of your work. Who else do you deal with?"

Gertrude sighed. "Lucy and Larry, when they're available."

"Oh," said Amanda again. She was at a loss for words. "There's the doorbell," she said in tones of relief. "It must be Don and Roderick."

Gertrude went to answer the door. She ushered Don and Roderick into the living room.

"What's up?" asked Gertrude.

Don sighed, and shook his head. "I couldn't get him

to go to bed. Every time I'd go to carry him upstairs he'd freak out."

"Freak out?" Gertrude frowned.

"Yeah, he'd scream and kick and fight me so that I had to put him down. I got him into bed once, but as soon as I'd read him his story and heard his prayers, he went crazy again. I thought I had him almost asleep that time, but as soon as I tried to creep out of the room he was wide awake."

"Did you ask him what was wrong?"

"He said that the pretty lady was going to come for him tonight, and he might have to go with her to Boston. I tried to convince him that it was all his imagination, but he insisted. So I asked him what I could do to help, and he said he wanted to come over here with you. By the way, who're Eddy and Freddy? He seemed to be talking about them this evening."

"Oh, I'm sorry Don, I should have told you. They're his guardians. Eddy's Larry's younger brother, and Freddy's his best friend. Molly got them assigned to guard Roderick."

"Well, all I can say is, I hope they're reliable. They didn't seem to be there this evening."

"I'm not sure that Roddy's aware of their purpose yet,"

said Gertrude. "I only just met them today myself, but if Eddy's anything at all like Larry, he's more than reliable. I'll check on them in a few minutes. In the meantime, come in and have a cup of tea with us."

"And the pretty lady kept calling to me," Roderick was saying as they returned to the kitchen. "I don't want to go with her, she hurted me." He took a bite of cookie.

"You don't have to go with her, sweetheart." Gertrude sat down next to him at the back of the table. "You don't ever go with anyone you don't know."

"I don't want to go with the man in the funny hat, either," said Roderick around his bite of cookie.

"Especially not him," said Gertrude, "and don't talk with your mouth full, please."

Roderick didn't reply. His bright blue eyes grew round with fear, and his mouth stayed open in mid-chew, as he stared out the window into the back yard. "Mommy, Mommy," he managed at last, "there goes the pretty lady." He pointed toward the back fence.

Everyone turned to look. A misty form stood in the

corner of the garden where the bushes had been cleared, staring down at the ground. Everyone watched in awe. At last she straightened her shoulders, and turned and floated along the fence, passed through it part way down the yard, and disappeared.

There was total, stunned silence in the kitchen for a few minutes. At last Jim said, "Wow, that's the most intense ghost I've ever seen!" He stared toward the back fence almost as round-eyed as Roderick.

"You told me you'd never seen one," said Mary Ann.

"No, I haven't and I didn't expect to either," said Jim.

Alec got up and pulled the curtains. "Maybe I shouldn't have cut down the shrubbery today. I wonder what's in that corner that fascinates her so?"

"Maybe she really did bury the family silver there," said Mary Ann. "Maybe that's why she went back to Boston."

"I don't know," said Gertrude, "but I'll bet we find out real soon."

"I can feel the energy gathering too," said Mary Ann. "I think this's going to be a busy night."

"If that's the case," said Jim, "I think we'd better finish our chores so that Amanda and Alec can go to bed."

"I can't stay," said Don, "I have office hours tomorrow. Can you look after Roderick and work too?"

"I guess so," said Gertrude. "He can keep watch with Jim if I have to do any trance work, and I'll check and see where Eddy and Freddy are before I start."

A half hour later the house had settled for the night. The three ghost hunters and Roderick took their accustomed places outside the maid's room.

"I'm going to check up on Eddy and Freddy," said Gertrude. "I'm not real sure about them yet." She quieted herself for trance, and presently found herself in the company of the two guardians.

"Games!" she exploded. "You two can sit there and play games while my son's in danger! You have a lot of nerve!"

The two spirits jumped, scattering cards everywhere. "It's just a friendly game of poker, mother, to while away the time," said Eddy.

"What were you doing when the pretty lady was trying to get him to go with her?" Gertrude's anger was at full boil.

"Pru can't take him with her, she doesn't have the strength. All she can do is call him," said Freddy.

"Nevertheless," said Gertrude, "your job is to protect my son. That means that you're on duty whenever he needs you, like this evening for instance. D'you know where he is right now?"

"Home in bed?" said Eddy.

"No he is not!" said Gertrude. "His father had to take him over here because the pretty lady was bothering him."

"Sorry, mother." Eddy's apology was feeble. "I guess we just didn't notice."

"We're new at this job," said Freddy.

"You'll not be at it long at this rate," said Gertrude. "I'm going to talk to Molly about this in the morning if not sooner. In the meantime you two will stand guard over my son like you're supposed to. Give me those cards."

"We can't," said Eddy.

"And why can't you?"

"Because they're spirit cards and you're not a spirit," said Freddy.

"Well, put them out of sight. I don't ever want to catch you playing cards on the job again!"

"Poker, indeed!" muttered Gertrude as she came out of trance.

"Poker?" asked Mary Ann.

"Those two excuses for guards were playing poker to while away the time," said Gertrude. "Oh, that makes me so angry. I intend to have a serious talk with Molly about this."

The night passed slowly. Roderick fell asleep leaning against Gertrude on the landing. "Poor little guy's exhausted," she said, looking down on her son. "I wonder if I can lay him down without waking him." She carefully moved Roderick to a reclining position beside her, and covered him with his 'blankie.' He stirred, and changed thumbs, and went back to sleep. "I'm glad Don thought to put his sleepers on him tonight," she said, "that way he won't be cold without a proper blanket."

Another hour passed. Roderick stirred, and seemed to waken. "Pretty lady," he muttered as he sat up and pulled his moist thumb from his mouth.

"Something's up." Jim roused himself from his state of relaxed alertness.

"I think I hear someone moving in Amanda's room," whispered Mary Ann.

Amanda's door opened and Amanda walked slowly down the hall toward them.

"She's sleep-walking again," said Gertrude. Roderick got up and took Amanda's hand. "Where're they going? I sure hope Eddy and Freddy are on the job."

"We're here, mother." The two voices echoed in unison in Gertrude's mind.

"The light's growing in the maid's room," said Jim, "and I can hear my machines going crazy." He rubbed his hands together gleefully. "This's going to be good."

"D'you want to trance this one," asked Mary Ann.

"Sure," said Gertrude, "if Jim'll keep an eye on Roderick in the physical."

"Anything you want," muttered Jim. He concentrated on the scene unfolding before him.

The two sensitives were soon in trance. Amanda and Roderick stood in the open doorway with Eddy and Freddy on either side of them. As they watched, the pretty lady slowly took form and moved toward Roderick with outstretched hands.

"Come to me, my child," she commanded.

"No," said Roderick, "you hurted me."

"Come, it will be all right, I won't hurt you again."

"No," said Roderick, "my mommy needs me, and I don't have to go with you."

"Who are you?" asked Amanda in a sleepy voice.

The apparition looked at her, startled. "Who are you?" she asked right back. "How did you get into Mrs. Archibald's house?"

"This's my house now," said Amanda. "I live here."

"Where's Mrs. Archibald?"

"She's dead," said Amanda.

"No, she can't be, I was just talking to her."

"What's your name?" asked Amanda.

"Prudence to you, and I want my baby. Come with me." She tried to take Roderick's astral hand.

"NO!" screamed Roderick pulling away from Prudence. "I won't go! I'm not your baby! I'm my mommy's little boy!" He turned and ran back to where Gertrude was observing the scene from the trance state.

Eddy and Freddy closed in on Prudence. She shrank visibly from their approach. "Save my baby!" she cried, then dissipated. The machines quieted their faint buzzing noises as Prudence's energy left the room.

"Wow!" said Jim. "I think we've got something here!"

Mary Ann and Gertrude stretched and stood up. Roderick attached himself to Gertrude's leg crying to be picked up.

"Mommy's here, darling, don't cry so."

"The pretty lady was here too." Roderick sobbed hard. "I saw her, and she wanted me to go with her."

"But you didn't go." Gertrude hugged him close to her. "You're my very brave boy, and I'm proud of you. She can't take you with her if you don't want to go."

"But I'm her baby! She told me so." Roderick's tears continued to run down his face and off his chin.

"No, you're not," said Gertrude. "You're my baby, and you just tell her that the next time she bothers you."

A noise attracted their attention to the maid's room. Amanda stood in the centre of the room with tears pouring down her face. "She wants my baby," she sobbed.

Mary Ann got to her first and put her plump motherly arms around her. "Hush, hush, Amanda. She can't take your baby from you. Come back to bed now, Alec's waiting." She guided the still sleeping Amanda toward her bedroom.

❖

"Well, this's been some night," said Jim in a whisper when they had reconvened on the landing to wait for dawn. "I wonder if there'll be any more disturbances? I can't wait to check out my recordings."

"I hope not." Gertrude sat on the top step and rocked a very drowsy Roderick to sleep. "There's been enough excitement for one night."

"What d'you suppose Prudence wants?" asked Mary Ann as she settled herself on the step below Gertrude.

"I think it's kind of obvious," said Gertrude. "She's looking for her baby, and she thinks Roddy's it."

"It seems to me she'd be willing to take anybody's baby," said Mary Ann. "Look at the effect she's having on Amanda."

"It was Prudence then, was it?" asked Jim who had only seen the physical side of the encounter.

Gertrude nodded. "Yes, she finally identified herself by name, and asked after Mrs. Archibald."

"So we have the right one, do we?"

"It seems so," said Gertrude.

CHAPTER 16

Gertrude sat at her kitchen table sipping her second cup of tea and trying to wake up. At least Roddy slept late this morning, she thought. He's having a good long nap now, too. Maybe I'd better wake him up, he'll never sleep tonight. She munched tiredly on a piece of cold toast. She looked at it in distaste, I don't even have the energy to make another one. She put her half eaten toast back on her plate, and finished her tea, which had also grown cold. She dragged herself to her feet and trudged wearily upstairs to get Roderick.

She stood for a moment looking down at the red curls and rosy face of her sleeping son. If anything ever happens to him… She pushed the thought away in a spasm of fear. I just hope that Eddy and Freddy are on their toes.

"We're here, mother." Eddy's voice echoed in Gertrude's mind.

You'd better be! she thought, not caring in her weariness, that she was being ungracious. She stroked Roderick's soft cheeks, and called his name. He stirred and opened his eyes.

"Mommy! You're here!"

"Where else would I be?"

"But I saw you a few minutes ago down by Sunday School."

"You must have been dreaming." Gertrude smiled. "Was it a nice one?"

"Very nice," said Roderick. "Mrs. Bolger was there." He struggled to sit up.

"D'you mean old Mrs. Bolger?"

"You know, Mrs. Granny." He rubbed the sleep from his eyes, and scrambled to the edge of the bed. "She wants you and me to come and have tea today."

"Oh, I don't think so," said Gertrude.

"Yes! Yes, she does!" said Roderick.

"Now dear, she's a very old lady, and she hardly knows

me. Why would she want us to come to tea?"

"She does! She does!" Roderick was on the verge of tears.

Gertrude sighed tiredly. "How about if I call her just to say hello, and if she really wants us to come to tea, she can ask me then."

"Okay," said Roderick. He jumped out of bed and began dressing haphazardly. Ultimately he had to stand still long enough for Gertrude to untangle his buttons and tuck his shirt in properly. In a few minutes he was downstairs at the kitchen table eating toast and peanut butter. "When are you going to call Granny Bolger, Mommy?"

"Right now, and don't talk with your mouth full please." Gertrude searched for Granny Bolger's number in the phone directory, and dialled. The phone rang interminably on the other end. I guess I'll let it ring a few more times, she's not very quick on her feet, she thought. Several rings later the receiver was lifted with a clatter. "Hello, Mrs. Bolger?"

"Hello, Gertrude," said the creaking old voice on the other end. "I was just going to call you. I've been thinking about you all morning."

"You have?" asked Gertrude.

"Yes, will you come and have tea with me? I've just made some sugar cookies, they're fresh out of the oven."

"Of course, we'll be glad to," said Gertrude. "What time would you like us to come?"

"Any time. Right now, if it's convenient. I have so much to talk to you about."

"We'll be right over as soon as I get Roderick dressed." A half hour later Gertrude and Roderick were eating sugar cookies with Granny Bolger. Her living room was packed full of ancient furniture, every one with a matched set of doilies on the arms and head rests. From a cage by the window a yellow budgie greeted them in the same tones that Mrs. Bolger had greeted them with when they came in. The heavy drapery was faded and formerly very dark in colour. Now it was a nondescript beige with hints of gold in the seams. It still occluded a lot of the daylight that would have shown up a patina of dust on all the flat surfaces.

"Amanda's Aunt Martha and I were good friends. We grew up together. I was acquainted with your mother too, you know." Mrs. Bolger filled Gertrude's tea cup and passed the cookies.

"No, I didn't know that," said Gertrude. "She never mentioned you."

"I went down to Boston to work and I got married down there. By the time my husband died, and I had moved back home, your mother had already moved to Texas. I was sorry to hear of her passing."

"Thank you," said Gertrude. "You said you had a lot to tell me?"

"Yes, I have some information you might be looking for."

"I don't know what that might be."

"Your mother and I kept in touch over the years. She told me about your gift. She said it was much stronger than hers. I have some of it too, although not very many people know about it. I've never used it commercially of course, just a hint to family and friends when necessary. I've saved a lot of people a lot of trouble over the years." Her wrinkled old face beamed happily at Gertrude. "You know I'll be ninety-nine my next birthday." Her faded blue eyes sparkled. "I remember a lot of stories from my youth. Have another cookie, dear." She passed the plate to Roderick and Gertrude.

"What are you trying to tell me, Mrs. Bolger?" Gertrude

absently took another cookie.

"My dear, you're very tired today," she said. "Your friend Amanda is having trouble at her house, is she not?"

"How do you know about that?" Gertrude frowned.

"I have my sources," said Granny Bolger. "I have some information you might need about that house."

"Oh," said Gertrude. "I'm glad someone has, we haven't had much luck finding it out from the library and the archives. What is it you want to tell me?"

"Now this is just gossip, dear. The whole business happened before my time, you understand. Well, not quite before my time, but I was very young, and I didn't hear the story until I was in my teens, some time later."

"I think I understand," said Gertrude. "You're saying that what you're about to tell me may be merely gossip and not quite accurate?"

"That's exactly it," said Granny Bolger with a happy smile. "The story goes something like this. Gordon Archibald was the son of a local businessman named Henry Archibald. Young Gordon was very bright and wanted to be a lawyer, so he went off to Halifax to study at Dalhousie. While he was there he met a young woman who was visiting friends. She was from Boston. He fell head over heels for her and when he was finished his studies he went off to Boston to marry her and bring her home to the Island. He built that great big house over there on Rochford Square where your friend Amanda lives, and they moved into it as soon as they were married. She was a wealthy young woman, and brought with her a cook and a maid. The maid is the one you're interested in."

"Go on." Gertrude held onto every word Granny Bolger spoke.

Granny refilled the tea cups and continued with her story. "The maid started stepping out with a young man of dubious reputation, and about a year later she was sent back to Boston. One can only surmise what must have happened, although there was nothing to prove it."

"What happened to the Archibalds?"

"She hired another maid, a local girl, and they lived in the house for about fifteen or twenty years. I remember that part because I used to walk by it every day on my way to school. Then Mrs. Archibald died. I don't know the cause, I was still quite young and they didn't discuss death and such things in front of children. He moved away then. I think he had an offer of a partnership up in Toronto. At any rate, he only came back to the Island in the summertime, and not every year, and never for very long."

"Do you know where Mrs. Archibald's buried?"

"Oh, I don't know." Granny Bolger shook her head. "I expect if she was buried around here she'd be in the old Protestant burying ground. Why?"

"No reason," said Gertrude. "I just thought it would be interesting to have a look at her gravestone. I'm wondering if she died in childbirth. What did Mr. Archibald do with the house?"

"It stood empty for quite some time until Amanda's uncle bought it when he got married to Martha. There were all kinds of strange stories circulating about the house by that time, and everyone was surprised when it was sold."

"What kind of stories?"

"Oh, the usual. You know the kind. The house was haunted, there were strange lights in it at night, there were apparitions in the garden. That sort of thing. Martha pooh-poohed the idea of ghosts, and she was never bothered by them."

"That sounds like Martha." Gertrude laughed. "She

didn't put up with much nonsense in the physical, and I don't suppose she'd have put up with anything from ghosts either."

"She was right not to, too. The only time she had any trouble in that house was when she was expecting. She blamed it on some neighbourhood boys up to pranks in the garden. She saw something down at the end of the garden where the old pump house used to be, and she went running down the yard. By the time she got there they'd already run away. All she found was a handkerchief caught on some bushes."

"I didn't know Martha had a baby," said Gertrude.

"She didn't," said Granny Bolger. "She miscarried at about twelve weeks. They were devastated. They very much wanted to have a family, but they never could. That's why she made so much of Amanda."

"I see," said Gertrude.

"Phew, I'm beat!" said Gertrude collapsing into a chair at Amanda's that evening. "You guys'll have to keep me awake until the fun begins."

"I'll help," said Roderick.

"I know you will, darling." Gertrude gave him a hug and a kiss. "You're very good at keeping Mommy awake."

"Did he have a restless sleep today?" asked Amanda.

"Not really. He just told me about his dream, which was rather interesting in that it came true almost immediately, and led to a very informative afternoon."

"What did you do?" asked Amanda.

"D'you remember Mrs. Bolger? She was a friend of your Aunt Martha's. She taught Sunday School for a few years after she came home from Boston."

"D'you mean Granny Bolger? She used to bring us the best cookies. Is she still alive? I thought she'd be dead long ago."

"Well, she's not dead, and she still bakes remarkable cookies, and she knew all about this house," said Gertrude.

"What about this house?" asked Alec.

"It's haunted, and has been almost from the first."

"I see," said Jim. "So did she say that the person we're looking for is Prudence Harrison?"

"She didn't call her by name, but I'm almost certain that's who she meant, because she's the one who came from Boston with Mrs. Archibald, and was returned in some haste a year later."

"Did she know why she went back to Boston?" asked Mary Ann.

"She hinted at something, but she didn't know for sure. She said that one could only surmise." Gertrude laughed. "She said she was keeping company, no, 'stepping out, with a young man of dubious reputation,' and was sent home shortly after that."

"Well, I guess it wouldn't be too hard to guess what might have happened," said Mary Ann. "D'you suppose she might have gotten pregnant? It would certainly explain her hang-up about babies."

"I suppose so," said Gertrude. "She also said that there were apparitions floating around in the garden in Aunt Martha's day, but Aunt Martha discovered they were boys up to pranks and chased them out."

"How'd she know it was just boys?" asked Amanda.

"She found a handkerchief caught on one of the bushes."

"Pure coincidence." Jim laughed. "Those naughty boys!"

"Maybe it isn't just pure coincidence," said Gertrude. "I was so tired this afternoon, I didn't make the connection until now, but Aunt Martha was pregnant at the time."

"But Aunt Martha never had any children," said Amanda.

"That's right, she didn't," said Gertrude. "She miscarried right after that."

"I don't like this one bit," said Alec, "not one bit! Aunt Martha only saw ghosts when she was pregnant, and miscarried immediately afterwards? I don't like it. What's going to happen to Amanda? I don't think I want you to continue with this investigation, Amanda. You may be the next one on Prudence's hit list."

"Now Alec, we talked about all this before," said Amanda. "You know the ghost doesn't appear if I'm not here, and we'll never get rid of it if we don't continue with the work right now. I'll be careful, and it's not as if I'm doing this by myself. Jim and Mary Ann and Gertrude are right there with me all the time. Besides, I don't think the ghost is really after me anyway."

"No, but she's after our baby, and you're the one who's carrying it, and she appears to have taken Aunt Martha's baby already. I'd like to know how many of Mrs. Archibald's children didn't make it to the real world because of her."

"Did Mrs. Archibald have children?" asked Amanda.

"No, she didn't, as far as Granny Bolger knew, but she didn't live a very long life either, so she could very well have died in childbirth."

"Did Granny Bolger know where she was buried?" asked Jim. "I'd like to get a look at the gravestone."

"She didn't know for sure. She thought it might be at the old Protestant burying ground on Great George Street. Something else interesting she told me was that the building at the end of your yard used to be a pump house."

"Hm," said Jim. "Pump house, eh. Well! I wonder if there's something hidden in the well?"

"Like what?" asked Alec.

"I keep telling you, the family silver." Mary Ann chuckled.

"Oh, be serious, Mary Ann, she wouldn't have hidden the silver in the well, she'd never have been able to get it back," said Amanda.

"Well, she's always yapping about babies, maybe she threw the baby down the well," said Alec. "Girls were always throwing their illegitimate babies in Government Pond to save themselves the disgrace of bearing a child out of wedlock, maybe she just chose the household well instead."

"That would've contaminated the well, wouldn't it?" asked Gertrude.

"Not if the well was no longer in use," said Alec. "I happen to know that there's another well on the property."

"Where?" asked Amanda. "I didn't know about it."

"It's at the other corner of the garden. I found it when I cleared away the bushes yesterday."

"D'you mean that pile of stones I thought was a wall is really a well curb?"

"The remains of one," said Alec. "It's all fallen in. There's only a depression about two feet deep left there now."

"For goodness sakes," said Amanda, "I'm amazed. All this time and I never knew there was a well on the property. Of course, I never went looking for one either."

"So if the maid had a baby and drowned it in the well, why's she haunting the upstairs?" asked Jim.

"Who knows?" said Mary Ann. "Maybe we should ask her, eh?"

"Or Molly," said Gertrude. "She's promised to find out about Prudence for me."

A few hours later the house had quieted for the night. "Wake me up when the fun begins." Gertrude yawned.

"Uh, uh." Mary Ann giggled. "You have to stay awake like the rest of us."

Gertrude groaned. "I'm so tired!"

"Napping isn't going to help any," said Jim, "and you're liable to miss something."

"Like what?" asked Gertrude.

"Like that." Jim pointed toward the maid's room where the light was getting brighter, and the machines were whirring and clicking in response to the growing energy.

Gertrude was instantly alert. Amanda came down the hall and took Roddy by the hand and led him to the door of the maid's room.

"Is she sleep-walking again?" whispered Mary Ann.

"I think so," said Jim.

"Don't waken her," said Gertrude softly, "I want to have a talk with Prudence if I can."

The light grew even brighter and spilled out over the group on the landing. Roderick stood as if asleep, with his hand in Amanda's facing the door.

If Prudence touches him I'll pound her! thought

Gertrude, ignoring the ridiculousness of the idea of pounding a ghost. She rose quietly from her seat on the top step and went to stand behind Roderick. The light grew brighter.

"She has a lot of power tonight," said Mary Ann quietly.

"Maybe we'll get something from her this time," muttered Jim under his breath.

"Sh!" said Gertrude.

"Bless you," said Prudence quite clearly. "Lemon and honey in hot water will clear that nasty cold."

"Thank you," said Gertrude. She was too startled to protest.

"I've come for you," said Prudence holding out her hand to Roderick. "I can't leave my baby behind a second time."

"What did you do with your baby in the first place?" asked Gertrude.

"Ding, dong, dell, my baby's in the well," said Prudence in a sing-song voice.

"Why's she in the well?"

"Because her Mommy fell." Prudence began singing a formless little tune just under the edge of her breath.

"Where did her Mommy fall from?" asked Gertrude.

"From grace," said Prudence staring hard at Gertrude.

"And now everyone can have babies except me."

"Is that why you want our babies?"

"I don't want hers," said Prudence pointing at the sleeping Amanda. "I want mine." She reached out her gossamer hand to Roderick.

Gertrude grabbed Roderick away from the reaching hand. "Well, you can't have him, he's mine."

"My baby-o, my baby-o, they sent me away from my baby-o," sang Prudence in a quavering soprano. She stopped singing abruptly. "And it was all because of that Angus!"

"What did Angus do?" asked Gertrude.

"Got me with child and then bragged about it," said Prudence. The ancient bitterness in her voice was almost palpable. "If he'd have kept his mouth shut no one would've ever known."

"How could you have concealed something like that?"

"I did. I'd already disposed of it before he opened his big mouth." Prudence began singing again. "Come with me my baby-o." She held out her hand to Roderick.

"Mommy! Mommy!" cried Roderick, dropping Amanda's hand, and climbing up Gertrude's leg in panic. "Don't let her take me!"

"Hush, Roddy," soothed Gertrude picking him up and holding him close. "She can't take you, you're mine."

"I want my darling baby-o," sang Prudence as she faded from sight.

Amanda sighed and walked back to her room.

"Wow!" said Mary Ann. "That's some story. I wonder if it's true?"

Gertrude sat down on the top step. "I don't know. It certainly could be, there was enough of that going on in those days."

"I wonder if Alec would be willing to dig up his back yard," said Jim. "We could look for bones, and that would show that at least part of her story is probably true."

"What would we do with the bones if we did find them?" asked Gertrude.

"We'd have to hand them over to the police, of course," said, "and I suppose a few explanations would be expected of us."

"More likely of Alec." Mary Ann giggled. "I wonder what he'd say?"

"That he was planting his garden and look what turnip?" Gertrude giggled too, giddy with fatigue.

"And how's he going to explain a garden that's been worked six feet deep?" said Jim.

CHAPTER 17

Gertrude and Roddy went out to Cherry Valley to visit Mary Ann the next afternoon. Her kitchen was as messy as ever and the kittens had learned how to get out of their box. Roddy lay on the floor pushing his truck around and shooing the kittens out of its path. Presently the truck noises stopped and Roddy had fallen asleep where he lay, with the kittens curled up beside him.

"I'm glad we called it quits early last night," said Gertrude. "I was exhausted. I don't think I'd have lasted until dawn."

"Me too." Mary Ann yawned. "Have another cookie." She passed the plate to Gertrude.

"No thanks, I'm cookied out." She nodded toward

Roderick. "Would you look at Roderick, he fell asleep on the floor playing with his truck."

"Poor little tyke didn't get enough sleep last night?"

"No, and it's warm in here with your wood stove still burning. He was still worried about Prudence when we got home, and it took me awhile to quiet him." She bent over to pick him up and gently deposit him on the couch. "Have you got a blanket?"

"Just fold the corner of the afghan down over him, it's plenty warm in here this morning."

"I wonder what news Molly has for me today?" said Gertrude. "She should have been able to scare up some information on Prudence by now."

"I'll mind Roddy if you want to trance," said Mary Ann.

"Thanks, you're on." Gertrude settled herself in the rocking chair, and turned her attention inward to find Molly sitting in her usual place on the clock shelf, Mary Ann's clock grinding and ticking beside her.

"It's time you got here," snapped Molly. "I've been sitting here for a half an hour! The blood's all run to my feet."

"What blood?" said Gertrude just as shortly. "And what feet?"

"You're getting too smart for your britches." Molly didn't like to be bested by a mortal.

"So what did you find out?"

"The baby's in the well, and Prudence was sent home to Boston," said Molly.

"I know that already. Whose baby was it?"

"Angus'. He conned her into thinking that he loved her and would marry her. You know, the usual story. The girls never learned, and there was nothing to protect them from their mistakes in those days."

"No, and they paid dearly for them too," said Gertrude. "Was it a boy or a girl?"

"It was a little girl. Ask Prudence about her, but don't take Roderick, he doesn't need to see this."

Gertrude sighed. "I wish he hadn't seen any of it."

"Oh, you needed him, for part of it at least," said Molly. "By the way, Slippery Jack Black has gone off to Boston for awhile, if you want to take Roddy to the park. You'll need to do it soon, though, because he'll be back for another round at the end of the week."

"Has he got anything to do with this?"

Molly shrugged. "Not much. He knew Angus, but they

didn't get along. They both wanted Prudence, but Jack was never here long enough to get her, so Angus had pretty nearly free rein with her. By the way, Jack was not a pirate in that lifetime. It was long past the age of pirates. He was just a very bad man."

"Would either of them have married her?"

"Angus might've, if she could've held out for it, but she was too lonely, and of course, once she was expecting he didn't want her."

"Of course not," said Gertrude scornfully, "they never did!"

"Well, they're not much better today," said Molly, "and the girls aren't any wiser either, for all their fancy sex education, and birth control devices."

"Is it worth our while to dig up the well?"

"I don't know. She was only a newborn, and her little bones would've been pretty soft. You might not find anything after all these years."

"Do you know how deep the well was?"

"About eight feet maybe. The water table's pretty high down there, lots of people get water in their basements when there's a lot of rain."

"Is there anything else I need to know?" asked Gertrude.

"Ask her to show you what happened that night. You might also ask her what she called the baby. Oh, and make sure that Eddy and Freddy are paying attention to Roderick when you do this."

"Thanks," said Gertrude, "I will."

"I hope this's the last night for this," said Gertrude from her usual seat on the top step at Amanda's house. "My bottom is taking a beating."

"Mine'll never be the same again, either." said Mary Ann. "I'll have a permanent ridge in it."

"Hush, you two, here comes Amanda," whispered Jim.

The door to the maid's room swung open and crashed against the wall as Amanda approached.

"Someone doesn't know her own strength." Mary Ann suppressed a giggle.

"Sh!" said Jim. "What can you see, Gertrude?"

"An angry Prudence," said Gertrude, rising from her seat and taking a place beside the drowsing Amanda in front of the open door. She focused her attention on the scene before her. The room took on its long ago appearance. Prudence was going through closets and drawers like a whirlwind, throwing clothing on the floor, and wherever else it would land.

"Damn that Angus!" said Prudence wrathfully. "Why couldn't he have kept his mouth shut? I had everything under control, and now I have to go back, and it's all because of him!" She began to cry.

"What's the matter, Prudence?" asked Gertrude softly.

"Oh, it's you again, is it?" She turned to look at Gertrude. "Did you bring my baby with you?"

"He's not your baby," said Gertrude.

"He was mine before he was yours, and I want her back."

"What do you mean?" asked Gertrude.

"Are you stupid or something? I just told you, your baby belongs to me."

"Why? You didn't look after her when you had her, and besides, my baby's a boy."

"So what! He was a girl when he was with me, and I want her back."

"Well, she's a boy now, and he's my baby, and I'm keeping him," said Gertrude. "What's Amanda's baby got to do with any of this?"

"I told you before, nothing. Amanda has strength."

"Why does Amanda have strength?"

"Because she's carrying."

"I see," said Gertrude. "So you don't want her baby."

"Of course not," said Prudence. "Her baby's nothing to me."

"What about Martha's baby?"

Prudence began folding clothing and packing them into a travelling bag. "Martha looked after my baby for awhile, but she gave her back to me."

"Can you show me what happened here that night?" asked Gertrude.

Prudence began to moan and hold her belly. "The pain was terrible!" She cried out in remembrance. "I couldn't make it stop." She moaned again as the scene shifted.

The cot in the corner took on a rumpled appearance, and Prudence's form lay in the middle of it, curled into a foetal position. Moans no longer issued from Prudence. The only indication of her agony was the regular stiffening of her back. Her anguished thoughts hung in Gertrude's mind.

I mustn't make a sound, Prudence thought wildly. No

matter how bad this gets I can't make one sound. She gritted her teeth against the next contraction. How long will it last, I wonder?

Gertrude stood listening to Prudence's thoughts and watching the birthing scene unfold for what seemed like hours. Prudence was making animal grunts with the strength of each contraction. Her lips were bleeding on the inside from her biting.

Soon, please God, soon, begged Prudence in her mind. At last it was over. She put the baby quickly to her breast to quiet its crying. It slept at last, and she rose shakily from her cot and cleaned herself. I'll just have to tell Mrs. Archibald that I had a heavy flow during the night, she thought. If I don't show her the worst of it she won't know the difference. She bathed the baby and dressed it in some clothing she'd been hoarding for these many months. She put the baby to breast again. I can't have you crying from hunger, she thought, gazing down at the tiny form in her arms. The baby hiccoughed I'll call you Rhoda. She smiled down at the now sleeping child. I'm sorry, I can't keep you, but this's the best for both of us. You can sleep in the attic today, and then I'll take you to Mother Baker, she'll find you a good home. She carried the baby up the attic stairs and laid her gently in a basket. "Now don't you cry, I'll be back to feed you by-and-by," she whispered.

The scene altered slightly. Gertrude knew time was passing by the subtle changes in the light. She could hear the baby crying.

Prudence hurried up the stairs to the attic. "Hush, Rhoda, hush. Oh, it's a good thing they're out for the day or they'd hear you." She fed the baby, and settled it back in its basket. "You look like him," she said gazing down at the infant which steadily returned her gaze. "Now, not a sound until I come again." She hurried back downstairs.

Darkness fell on the past, and Gertrude stood entranced, watching as Prudence tried unsuccessfully to quiet the screaming infant.

"Hush, Rhoda, they'll hear you," she said.

"Prudence!" called a woman's voice from downstairs. "What's going on up there? Is that a baby I hear?"

"No, ma'am," said Prudence covering up the mouth of the wailing infant with her hand. "It's just a toy I picked up at the market today. I'm going to send it to my nephew in Boston."

"Well, stop playing, and come down here, I need you."

The baby struggled against Prudence's quieting hand and then lay still. Prudence looked down in horror at the dead infant in her arms. "Oh, Rhoda, what have I done to you? My baby! What am I going to do?"

Prudence hastily wrapped the tiny corpse in a blanket and stuffed it into a carpet bag, then turned and hurried downstairs.

The scene darkened to night as Gertrude watched. Presently Prudence appeared in the attic again. A set look of determination was on her face.

"It's time Rhoda," she whispered, as she pulled the stiffened little form from its hiding place. "I've found the perfect place to put you." She wrapped the blanket more securely around the baby and carried it downstairs. Gertrude's mind seemed to follow her as she carried her little burden to the end of the garden. Prudence's thoughts sounded clearly in her mind.

It's lucky for me the pump house blew over and wrecked the well curb in the storm last winter, she thought. If it hadn't the skunk would have never fallen in and contaminated it, and I would never have had a place to put you, my darling. This's not a very good grave, but it will have to do, and at least you'll not have to share it, like you would if I put you in the pond. I'm glad now that I didn't tell Mother Baker about you, she's one less person to know. She stood holding the baby for a few more minutes. "Goodbye, my darling," she said at last and hurled the baby to the bottom of the well.

Back on the landing, the splash startled Gertrude out of trance. "I can't believe what I just saw!" she gasped. "I just can't believe it! No wonder she's looking for her baby!"

Amanda turned and wandered back to her room.

"What happened?" asked Mary Ann and Jim in the same breath.

"She smothered it and threw it down the well!"

"Good grief!" said Jim. "Now, I suppose we really will have to dig up the well in order to put Prudence to rest."

"Maybe not," said Gertrude. "We could always give the baby a proper funeral, bless it, and send it back to Prudence. It's worth a try at least."

"And a lot less messy than digging up the back yard," said Mary Ann. "Who'll we get to do the service?"

"Someone who's not too orthodox," said Jim. "We may have to go off the Island to get someone."

Gertrude shook her head. "What's the matter with us doing it? We can pray just as well as any minister, and it needn't be a full-fledged funeral service, it can just be a memorial."

"It's worth a try," said Mary Ann, "and we may put Prudence to rest tonight."

"Let's go for it," said Jim. "The sooner we do it, the sooner Amanda's out of danger. Who'll do the praying?"

"I will," said Gertrude. "C'mon, let's go down to the garden."

They trouped out into the night. A salt breeze from the harbour stirred the trees. Overhead a three-quarter moon added its glow to the light from the milky way. A dog barked nearby and then was silent, as if aware of their mission.

They arranged themselves around the old well site, and bowed their heads. A bird chirped sleepily from a branch above their heads.

"Dear Lord," began Gertrude, "receive this little child to your care tonight. Be with Prudence, and help her find rest and comfort with her infant. Pardon her sins of omission and commission. May they rest in peace with You forever. In Jesus' name we pray, amen."

The little group stood in silence for a moment, then all turned as one and trooped back to the landing. The light from the maid's room was softer now. Gertrude and Mary Ann looked inside. Prudence sat in the rocking chair nursing her baby. An expression of contentment smoothed the anger and unhappiness from her face. She looked up at Gertrude, smiled, and said quite clearly, "Thank you," and faded from sight.

The sun was just breaking the horizon when they finished packing up the equipment.

"Another successful mission completed," said Jim.

"It's so satisfying to have helped ease another's burden," said Gertrude.

"Not only that, I have a ton of readings to analyze and write up. I'll get at least three papers out of this, and maybe some magazine articles. I wish I could write fiction, I'd have a book too." Jim yawned. "But not tonight."

Alec appeared on the stairs and called down to them, "D'you guys want some breakfast before you go? We're just getting up."

"Sounds good to me," said Mary Ann, "What about you two?"

"I could use some," said Gertrude. "It's been a long night and Don won't be expecting me home for at least another hour."

A knock sounded softly on Amanda's front door. Roderick's childish voice said in a loud whisper, "Maybe they're still in bed."

Gertrude opened the door, and Roderick hurled himself at her in a fierce bear hug. "You two are early birds this morning," she said.

Don nodded. "Yes, Roderick had a very restless night, full of dreams. I don't know why he's so full of pep now."

"The pretty lady's gone now, isn't she, Mommy," he said.

"Yes dear, we found her baby for her, and she went away with it. She doesn't need to be here any more."

"I'm glad for that." Amanda joined them in the downstairs hallway. "I was beginning to be afraid that we really would have to move out."

"I'll put the kettle on." Alec headed toward the kitchen.

A half hour later they relaxed in Amanda's kitchen, with the comfort of full stomachs, and the satisfaction of the completed project.

"So Roddy was actually Prudence's child that time, eh?" asked Don.

"It would seem so," said Gertrude, "but I thought you didn't believe in reincarnation."

"I don't, didn't," he said. A look of confusion crossed his face. He sighed. "Living with you has taught me that anything's possible."

"So d'you believe in it now?" Mary Ann was sitting on the kitchen lounge with her stockinged feet curled up under her and leaning with her elbow on the raised head of the lounge.

"I'm not committing myself," said Don. "It's too deep a question, and nothing can be proved. However, I'll keep an open mind."

"It was interesting that Prudence could only appear when there was a pregnant woman in the house, wasn't it?" said Amanda.

"Yeah," said Mary Ann, "she seemed to draw power from

you even though she couldn't draw it from us."

"D'you suppose it was because her experience centred so firmly around pregnancy and delivery and babies, that she looked for that kind of power exclusively?" asked Jim.

"I don't know," said Gertrude, "it could be the reason. I'm just thankful she didn't get to Roddy."

"He's an amazing kid," said Jim. "How many children his age would stand up to a ghost the way that he did?"

"Could she have taken Roderick?" Don's brow creased with worry again.

Gertrude shook her head. "No, she didn't have the power, and besides, she was from an alternate reality so she couldn't have, no matter how much she wanted to."

"I wonder whatever became of her after she was sent back to Boston?" asked Don.

"Molly told me about that the other day. She said that she got a job as a housekeeper to a wealthy family in Boston by forging references. She stayed there for about ten years until it all finally worked on her mind and she hanged herself in the root cellar one day."

"Poor thing!" said Mary Ann.

"I wonder why she haunted this house, and not the

house in Boston?" said Alec.

"Well, we don't know that she didn't haunt the house in Boston," said Gertrude, "but I would say that it's probably because her baby was here that she held on here for so long."

"There's one thing I don't understand about all of this," said Don. "If Roddy is the reincarnation of Rhoda, why could we hear Rhoda crying in the house?"

"It was only the psychic impression of Rhoda's crying that we were hearing, like a tape recording," said Gertrude. "Her true spirit had re-entered the physical in Roderick. That's why Prudence was able to home in on him as her baby."

"Well, what was Prudence?"

"Somewhat imprudent." Mary Ann giggled.

Gertrude glared in her friend's direction. "She was an unhappy spirit with a lot of unfinished business in the physical, and until she could finish her business here, she couldn't move on. By releasing her baby to God, and praying for her forgiveness, we allowed her to do that."

"Are you guys satisfied that she's gone now?" asked Jim of Amanda and Alec.

Amanda and Alec exchanged searching glances with one

another. "I think so," said Amanda. "There seems to be a lightness in the atmosphere here that wasn't here yesterday. A clearness, so to speak."

"I agree with Amanda," said Alec. "I feel as if we're free now."

"Yes, I just feel as if everything's going to go smoothly to the end," said Amanda. "I have this happy picture in my mind of us carrying our baby down to be baptized at Zion."

"Are we invited?" asked Gertrude.

"Of course," said Amanda, smiling sunnily, "you're going to stand with us."

"Meow," agreed Kitty, appearing from nowhere, as was her habit.

Also by Margaret A. Westlie

Scottish Pioneers

Mattie's Story

Mattie Cameron is only 15 years old. Her mother wants her to marry a man whose name she doesn't know--that very day.

Anna's Secret

Anna is dead. How does the close and caring community solve her murder without detectives?

An Irregular Marriage

Annie's parents are gone. Her sweetheart is absent. Where will she find a home?

Partners Paranormal

Shades of Molly

Who ever knew astral travel could be so much fun? Join Molly as she helps her nemesis discover her psychic gifts and find romance.

Molly and Company

Who better to help on a ghost hunt than a ghost who is your friend? Molly is back, riding herd on an unruly spirit, while her ghost-hunting friends investigate his house.

Partners Extraterrestrial

Another Way of Being

Advena wants to feel like a human. Jim needs to think like an alien. Maybe human and alien are not so different after all.

www.ingramcontent.com/pod-product-compliance
Lightning Source LLC
Chambersburg PA
CBHW071828020726
47502CB00004B/1280